CHRONIC FAITH

BASED ON A TRUE STORY

MATTHEW LEMKE

CONTENTS

This book is dedicated to the amazing warrior Christina Doherty
Along with all EDS, Chiari, and Cystic Fibrosis fighters.
Special thanks to all those who assisted in helping me create this book. To
my editor, Ginger Shoup, you did such amazing work making this book
easier to read! To my beautiful wife, thank you for always supporting me
in this crazy adventure of life. You continue to push me to be a better man
and now a father to our children. Finally, thank you to Nathan Rodriguez
for the amazing artwork of the book cover!
Before we dive into this book, I'd like to start with a prayer...
Father God,

*I pray for the reader to gain something from you in this story that you have
blessed me with. I ask you to use these words for you own and not of mine.
Please help me keep a pure heart and never get caught up with how many
books that I sell. Guide me in remembering it's solely about peoples' hearts
and not about the money I make. God, I pray that if 1,000 people buy this
book that at least 1 person is touched by you. Amen!*

INTRODUCTION

What will you do when you are facing the biggest obstacle of your life? It will come down to two choices: give in to fear or seek the path of faith. Fear looks like the easier and more tempting path. You see a horrifying monstrosity on your path? Fear tells you to turn around and take the easier way. But choosing faith typically requires a heck of a lot of courage because you know that if you fail, you'll fail *hard*. I will forever remember the day I had to make that choice. It was the day I was empowered by the knowledge that God is entirely faithful to us...that when we are struggling through the most difficult challenges, God can make the biggest changes in our hearts. If we lived a life of sameness and never faced storms, how would we grow?

The title *Chronic Faith* came to me as I was writing this book and reflecting on my chronic illness and the results that came from having just about everything thrown at me. *Chronic* means over a long time or recurring, and *faith* means a strong belief or trust. Things that are *chronic* typically refer to bad things: crippling conditions that people have to endure for a long time. But *chronic* could also mean something different: something that helps us grow over time. Maybe something that is *chronic* can be a tool in our bag of things to empower us.

So, when I say that you should have "chronic faith," I mean that you need to have a long-lasting and growing faith. Whenever I tell people my story and the jaws begin dropping, they sometimes ask me, "How can you smile when talking about how much you went through?" It's a great question because I probably seem like a crazy person. The answer is simple: because, even today, after all that I've been through, God still pursues me.

This book (and my previously published memoir) isn't a magical fix. Your problems won't vanish when you finish reading this. But if even one person turns their perspective into a positive mindset after experiencing my story, I feel that I've been successful. And I encourage you to share your story with others too for the same reason. Don't ever feel discouraged to share your beautiful story. Tell people how you prevailed with a little bit of faith, some hard work, and a positive mindset.

As you read this story, you may laugh, feel shocked, and even cry, knowing that it is based on what happened to me.

CHAPTER 1

*Beep...Beep...*Benjamin slowly opened his blue eyes with the strange sensation that he had slept for days but had somehow arrived in a new century. Only his eyes moved as he scanned the room, finding a tall machine next to his bed that was making the piercingly loud beeping noise that must have awakened him. He followed the lines from the machine to his chest and discovered clear plastic over his face, and he was suddenly aware of how uncomfortable it was. It took him a moment to realize that it was an oxygen mask, but regardless of what it was, the feeling of overwhelming claustrophobia that overcame him demanded that he remove it. He grunted as he tried with all his strength to reach it with his hands, but for some reason, he could not achieve this simple task. His arms wouldn't come up. He wondered whether they were strapped down. The effort seemed to exhaust him though, and as he felt anesthesia overcome his system again, he slipped back to sleep.

Benjamin Norwood didn't find out he had a chronic illness until he was 23, but he had always known in his gut something was wrong. He had hidden small problems from his family and told himself the pain was normal. He might have prayed for God to help him except that he had never truly seen God as a guiding force despite growing up in a Christian household. Somewhere along the way, he had come to the conclusion that he was alone and that all his problems were solely his to deal with.

Perhaps it had to do with having been bullied constantly and how he had never learned to ask for help or stand up for himself. Instead, he had shouldered on, suffering in silence. When people said he was weird, he ignored them or tried to laugh it off. When people made fun of the way he looked, he pretended not to hear. He avoided approaching people and tried to fade into the background.

Ben was raised in southeast Texas on a small ranch about 20 minutes from a city called Victoria. Working cattle and throwing square bales, he grew up learning what hard work could achieve. However, living so far from the city had certain drawbacks. For one, he and his two siblings had to be up at about five-thirty in the morning to catch the bus for school. For another, it was more difficult to make friends since there weren't any kids for miles around his house. It was especially hard for kids like Ben, who had learned that the best way to avoid rejection and teasing in school was to stay quiet. On the long bus ride each day, he would find an empty seat, lay his head against the window, and close his eyes. Sometimes, the rumblings of the engine lulled him to sleep. When it didn't, he pretended he was asleep so that no one would take notice of him.

One rainy day, just when then 11-year-old Ben was settling in for a nice fake nap, a boy came and sat next to him. There was a bit of an awkward silence as Ben, with eyes closed, tried to decide what to do.

And then the boy, who apparently was not fooled by the act, said, "My name is Brandon! It's nice to meet you. Do you want to play with my Star Wars figures?"

After a pause in which he reluctantly gave up his ruse, Ben opened his eyes at last and gazed in wonder at the strange creature who had invaded his solitary world. Then a spark ignited within Ben, and something he hadn't even realized had been there was awakened. He exclaimed, "Dude, I actually love Star Wars!"

They were instant best friends and soon started telling people that they were brothers. One day, they made a pact together. "When I get married, you're going to be my best man," they promised each other.

The thought of one day getting married and having a family was an exciting thought for Ben. When he had a crush on a girl, he often imagined the far future and marriage rather than the more immediate romance. And despite his usual avoidance of others, Ben once found himself pursuing a relationship with a seemingly kind-hearted girl in his grade named Allison, but she never responded favorably. It seemed even she didn't want to be associated with the weird kid.

Rejection was a familiar thing for him, and he sometimes spiraled into deep episodes of depression. But he never asked for help or showed his feelings to anyone. Even his parents, who were caring and attentive, had no idea of his suffering. He had become a master at hiding his emotions. It worked quite well against bullies. He had only to act bored, and they usually moved on.

Eventually, after he had gained confidence from his friendship with Brandon, he also learned the art of making others laugh, and he shifted away from being the quiet weirdo and became the class clown instead. But it was just another type of wall to protect himself from others.

The thing about suffering from a mental illness is you either let it completely drive your life or learn to cope with it. But coping with it alone is not smart. Ben continued to push forward during the depressing times of his life by smiling and not letting others enter his heart. Ben suspected that Brandon had noticed his moods changing and had understood that there was a darker layer to Ben's existence, but Brandon never brought it up. He continued to be his friend no matter what mood Ben was in. He invited Ben over to his house for sleepovers and late-night video games. Brandon never knew how much his friendship meant to Ben or the impact it was having. Having just the one close friend was enough to keep Ben stable.

One morning, upon waking for school, 13-year-old Ben sat up in bed and flung his legs over the side. As he gave his pillow one last look of longing and prepared to stand, an excruciatingly sharp pain shot from his right foot, up his leg, and into his lower back. But this did not alarm him at all. He simply stretched, convinced himself that he must have slept on it funny, and proceeded with his usual schedule. The pain continued intermittently throughout the day, but he found relief by limping and putting most of his weight on his left leg.

At school, the kids instantly noted this new physical impairment, and Ben heard them say, "He walks like a gangster!" Ben took this as a form of acceptance from his peers and continued to limp because it felt good to be noticed for more than just his physical appearance or being the weird kid. Now he had a cool walk. Awesome. It helped alleviate the depression a bit.

The other thing that helped that school year was the start of a passion for theater. He joined an after-school club of competitive theatric poetry, and he was flooded with excitement and hope for all the possibilities in this new adventure. Going out of town to compete in theater tournaments became a form of therapy, especially when he discovered he had a knack for it. He was thrilled to find himself excelling at acting, and he supposed it was all the emotions that he had compressed away exploding out all at once in his performance.

One day in class, his theater teacher presented a once-in-a-lifetime chance that would turn Ben's life completely upside down. "Okay, class, today I received an email from our local theater. They will be holding a contest called "Finding the Stars." If you'd like to enter, you will have to prepare a one-minute monologue. The person who gets first place will win a drama scholarship at our community college and a signed contract with a talent agency."

After class, she took Ben aside. "You're going to enter, right?"

Ben nodded.

"Good! You have real talent. I can't wait to see what you can do with this!"

Benjamin went home that day, excited to share the news about this opportunity to become a signed actor. Getting off the bus, he noticed that his troublesome leg had worsened. His little brother and sister noticed it and begged him to tell their parents. The pain was greater, and he found that he was unable to press his heel all the way down. The concern that his siblings showed was finally a red flag for him, and he brought this up to his parents along with the exciting news.

Monday came around, and he was taken out of school that day to see the family doctor. He prepared his story of what had been going on and comforted himself with the knowledge that the doctor would figure it out.

After hearing everything, the doctor's response was, "I'm not sure what's going on, but let's get you an X-ray for your hip. And here is a prescription for the pain."

Ben anxiously waited for the phone call from the doctor's office that would bring him the answer—whether it was some small injury that would heal soon or...something else. A few days later, he eavesdropped on the call to his mother. "Hi, I am calling about Benjamin's hip X-rays. There was nothing abnormal, so the doctor says he is okay."

Ben decided that if the doctor was not concerned, he would not be concerned either. He began preparing for "Finding the Stars" and chose to ignore the pain that had become a normal part of his life.

And the day finally came for his chance to become the actor he had dreamed of. He got there several hours early to do practice runs with his theater teacher, and boy, did he realize how much he was unprepared. He had practiced more than a dozen times before, but now he was having trouble remembering it all. He wasn't sure whether it was another symptom of health problems or just due to the nervousness he felt.

As he waited just off stage, hearing the audience clapping for the previous contestant and knowing that he would be standing alone with a spotlight on him in front of a hundred or more people with a half-memorized monologue, he could just about hear his heart coming out of his chest. He was shaking in fear. However, the moment he stepped out, it was like someone flipped a switch, and all the nervousness just completely left his body. Ben performed his monologue so flawlessly that he received a standing ovation. As he waited for the judges' decision, several other contestants whispered that they thought he would win. One even congratulated him on getting first place.

The awards ceremony came shortly after his perfect performance, and he found himself back on the stage, lined up with the others. After third place was awarded to a girl who had recited a poem about whales, the announcer called, "Second place goes to Benjamin Norwood!" Several people were surprised he hadn't gotten first place, and Ben felt the dream slipping away. He wouldn't get the scholarship or contract. But he was used to rejection and disappointment by now. So, he pasted a smile on his face and accepted his second-place trophy.

After first place was awarded to a boy who had spoken about a hilariously disastrous camping trip he had taken with his family, Ben began to limp off with his family out of the building. But then the theater director was chasing them down, yelling, "Wait! Don't leave yet!" Once he had caught up with them, he said, slightly out of breath, "One of the agents who were watching would like to talk with you about signing a contract." Ben's family started to freak out, thinking something big was about to happen. And they were right.

His sister looked over to him saying, "Bubba! You're gonna' be famous!"

Ben nervously chuckled and looked down to his little brother who was holding his hand out for a fist pound. He reached out slowly, and they both made explosion noises.

Even through all the excitement that followed over the next few weeks, Ben noticed that he now was beginning to experience joint pain all over his body. He also became unusually flexible. He could put both his legs behind his head with ease even though he had never been able to do that before. But with every step he took, his right knee popped. So, when he walked quickly, it sounded like a bunch of Pop Rock candy exploding. And when he was standing, his knee was hyperflexed and therefore offsetting his center of gravity. The sharp pain in his leg sometimes became throbbing. He told his parents it was still hurting, and they took him back to the same doctor several times. Each time, the doctor expressed a variation of the same thing: he was fine. Once, the doctor seemed to be arguing that Ben *couldn't* be having a serious problem because he was young and had no family history of related problems. His recommendation? Exercise. So, Ben just gritted his teeth and continued to push forward, and he had no idea what this decision would do to his life.

CHAPTER 2

High school is a major transition for any teenager, but for Ben, with his declining health and newfound acting career beginning to bloom, there never seemed to be enough time or energy to fully take in the new sights and feelings. There was enough for old pursuits, however. Allison was the prettiest girl in school and was often seen surrounded by boys seeking her attention. Ben hoped that his potential of being a film actor would give him an edge with her. But when this did not work, he finally decided that he would just have to trust that true love would happen in God's timing and that the key was patience.

Meanwhile, his acting career didn't require much patience. He got a call from his agent informing him that he had the biggest audition of his life for a feature film as a co-star with his celebrity crush Selena Gomez. He was filled with a mixture of sickening nerves and giddy anticipation. So, a few days later, his mother came to pick him up early from school, and they raced to Austin, the so-called "Hollywood of Texas," rehearsing his lines the whole way.

One of the things going for him was that he had done several auditions already for this casting director and had developed a friendship with her.

That didn't stop the nerves he felt as he walked into a small room. Beads of sweat were trickling down his back, and he tried to slow his breathing. The casting director noticed immediately that he was not his normal confident self and gave him the pep talk he needed.

She said, "Ben, you have auditioned for me many times, and I love your attitude and courage! You have the perfect look for this role, but I'm going to need you to breathe and relax. Do you need a minute? Would you like some water?" He nodded his head and smiled gratefully. After a few minutes of casual talking and drinking water, he felt himself relaxing enough to perform.

He nailed the audition and walked out feeling absolutely confident about it. Now he just had to wait, which, in some ways, was worse than auditioning. It was a highly stressful few weeks, but a time in which he learned a lot about the film industry. He finally got the call from his extremely excited agent, telling him that he in fact booked the role! After days of negotiating his contract, they signed the deal.

His mother then went to his school the following day to withdraw him and begin the process of homeschooling him since he was still a sophomore. Filming started several months after this in Dublin, Ireland, which was the first time Ben had been out of the country.

"Mom, I still can't believe we are flying to Ireland to film a movie with SELENA GOMEZ!" he exclaimed as they reached the airport. His mother was also ecstatic as she boarded the plane, reminding Ben that this was her second time to go there. She was a huge fan of Ireland, and if she could have had it her way, she would have lived there permanently.

Benjamin performed amazingly and became very close with everyone in the cast and crew. And, although he stayed grounded and humbled most days, he had his moments when it was hard to not have a level of cockiness about what he was doing. But it was hard to feel too superior when he couldn't walk without pain. During his time on set, plenty of people took note of his limping, and after long days of filming, walking became nearly unbearable. He didn't sleep well at night, and he was tired all the time. And one day, he found that he was no longer able to take full deep breaths.

He decided not to tell anyone because he thought that they would make a such a fuss about it that it would mess up the filming. After a few months, he and his mother came back home to a welcoming party. Everyone was so proud of him.

Ben continued to hide his new and worsening health issues from his family, but his mother noticed them one day at dinner and insisted they see the doctor again. Ben agreed rather reluctantly. He had learned, like many others seeking help, that physicians often prefer to dismiss patients' concerns as hypochondria, attention seeking, or attempts to fulfill drug addictions. Yet here he was once again, being sent home from his doctor with the idea that exercise and stretching would fix everything, which of course, proved futile.

He was soon back in public school, and at the end of his senior year, he had become very popular with everyone in town. He highly enjoyed all of the attention and finally felt accepted by his peers. No one called him the weird kid anymore.

Soon after graduating, he was pleased to find himself living in Austin. But several months of landing a few small-time gigs here and there never seemed to get his feet going in the right direction. He was in a bit of a rut. The movie he had played in was fantastic, and he had enjoyed it immensely, but now that he had achieved such success, it almost felt like he was done—like he had already reached his goal, and he didn't know where to go next. He even turned down a few auditions when they didn't feel right. He played with the idea of getting into photography, but he was wishy-washy about that too. He felt the true purpose for his life was just around a corner and he was going in circles to find it.

While trying to make up his mind, he biked to his job at McDonald's and could never save enough money to get a reliable vehicle. He often spent his earnings on non-essential things such as video games or eating out all the time. Within six months, he had run out of savings with nothing to show for it, and with the resolution of defeat, he moved back to his parents' home. Maybe it was simply accepting failure, but he thought it was far better than living on the streets.

Ben was bitter with God for this disappointment in what he had considered his calling, but mostly, he was upset with himself for making what he felt were the wrong decisions. But God works in mysterious ways, which was something Ben would learn much later. Once he got home, he moped around the house with his head hanging low for a few weeks. He made no effort to look for a job and spent his time playing video games and taking pictures of animals and flowers.

Finally, his parents sat him down and gave him a stern "parent talk" about adult responsibility. "You always have a place to stay with us here, but we hope one day you'll get on your own feet. So, that means that you need to be either enrolled in college or working somewhere to further yourself," his father said.

"Since the acting career seems to have fizzled out," his mother added, "we strongly encourage you to find work in the oilfield business. It's really profitable and easy to get into."

"I'm not really interested in that," Ben responded. "I'm going to find a job as a server or something like that so that I can still pursue acting. It's what I really want to do. I can do it. I just need to get a good break again." As he said this, he wondered whether he really believed it himself.

Though they seemed supportive of him at least having a plan, he could tell they were not really on board with his pursuit of what they called a "lottery type of dream." This added more to his doubts.

He kept his promise and began applying for local jobs. Soon, he was selling camera equipment and computers with the hope that he'd get more auditions, but nothing came. After a few weeks of this fast-paced work, his breathing sometimes became so difficult that he felt he might pass out. He pushed aside his feeling that he had not been taken seriously by the doctor and convinced himself that the doctor must know best after all. Every day, he told himself, "I'm fine, and there is no need to be worried! The doctors have checked me several times and told me I'm okay."

And he found more excuses to ignore his health. For example, he reasoned that since he was living in a society that values men who are tough and uncomplaining, he would never be looked at as a real man if he gave too much voice to his suffering. That is how he continued to put his health in the back seat.

Chapter 3

Ben was now twenty-two, and though he lived rent-free with his parents, he never managed to save anything. He spent his money on things he wanted, never able to resist buying the things he could but perhaps shouldn't. He had built a nice cache of quality camera equipment and fed his addiction to expensive coffee nearly every day.

One day, Ben received a phone call from his old buddy, Brandon. After high school, they had become distant and only occasionally connected on social media. So, when he saw Brandon pop up on his caller ID, it took him by surprise. Ben recognized his voice as Brandon said, "Hey man, I'm sorry I haven't gotten back to you in so long. Life got really busy, and I joined the military. I just got out of boot camp a few weeks ago."

Ben was in complete shock. How had he not known that his best friend had made such a huge commitment? His next reaction to this news was worry for his brother's safety. "What if he gets deployed to some war and dies?" he thought to himself as Brandon told him what his training had been like. Then, as Brandon went on about getting stronger and more confident and feeling like he had a purpose in life, Ben realized that the risks Brandon was facing might be worth it for that feeling of being in the right place–especially at this point in

Ben's life when he was clinging to what seemed to be a dying dream. If Brandon had found another purpose, why couldn't he?

If only he could figure out what that purpose was. Since he was always in pain, he had felt he would never have the chance. But this phone call had given him a new idea. Getting stronger could mean that his body might overcome whatever was bothering it. The plan gained energy when Brandon told him how amazing the benefits were for joining the military. For instance, he could get college paid for. Despite the fact that Ben had just been imagining his friend being blown up in battle, he listened avidly. Perhaps like a drowning man reaching for a shiny new cardboard box, he latched onto the idea.

After he and Brandon had disconnected, Ben decided the next thing to do was to seek guidance from his Grandfather Smith, who had served more than thirty years in the Marines, flying jets and building his rank to Gunnery Sergeant.

When he had explained his desire, his Grandad replied, "The military is a huge commitment, but I think it's a fine idea!"

Ben smiled. "But Grandad, I'm not sure what branch to go with."

"I strongly suggest you do not join the Army. They are a bunch of uncivilized children who can't follow orders."

Ben knew that Grandad was of the "old Marines," who were known to have an especially high disregard, even disdain, for the Army.

After a two-hour lecture of the pros and cons of each branch, Ben narrowed it down to the Coast Guard or the Marines. As for specific roles, Ben had two ideas. One was based on advice that he should get a job in the military that could correspond to a job in the real world, like engineering, cooking, or photography. Ben jumped on the idea of becoming a combat photographer. His side hobby could become a career! Ben contemplated that perhaps he had finally found God's plan for him.

Three weeks later, he was sworn into the Marines to become a combat photographer. During his medical checkup and while filling out medical history paperwork, Ben felt it wasn't necessary to bring up his health issues since they weren't real enough for doctors anyway. He even did his best to not limp or show any signs of pain in front of anyone. The recruiter informed him before finishing all the official paperwork that basic training would consist of 13 weeks of extreme conditions.

He would be sent to San Diego, California on August 1st, which gave him a month to get things prepared and say goodbye to his loved ones. Ben was a little bothered when several of his family members told him that he would be a completely different man the next they saw him, but he reminded himself that the change was needed—that this was his last option for having a productive life. Even though doubts sometimes crept up on him when he was alone, it was too late to change his mind since he had signed the dotted line on the unbreakable contract.

So, despite all these fears that tried to consume him, he began packing for a major life shift in a direction God had set for him. Ben lay in his bed staring at the ceiling for hours, getting lost in his thoughts. Finally, he fell deep asleep, and dreams found him.

He was standing at a podium. There were hundreds of people clapping excitedly for him. He began speaking in a preacher-like voice. There was firm authority in it. "Fear is a thing that comes into someone's life to try to control it," dream Ben said. "A warrior does not have to live with the absence of fear. The warrior lives a life of courage by converting the fear into faith. Think of it like this...Your life is a car, and the choice of fuel that drives your car is up to you. Faith is premium, and fear is regular, so which one is going to be better for your engine? Which one will keep you going longer and in better condition? The answer is premium. The answer is faith."

He awoke from his dream the next morning feeling incredibly motivated and positive. He wondered whether it was God and not himself who had been speaking at the podium. Ben kept this unusual dream to himself. It felt too personal to share, like it was meant just for him. With this new energy, he threw himself full force into conditioning for boot camp in the short time that he had.

On the morning of August 1st, he and his family left for the Austin airport, which was a two-hour trip. Most of the way, they exchanged funny stories and reminisced about good times. They didn't talk about how much they were going to miss him. But toward the end of the drive, his little brother, Brenner, who was eight, said, "Please don't die while you're in the military, Bubba." After this, the car ride was mostly silent. Ben suspected they were all brewing on the danger Ben was going into.

Once they got to the airport, there were plenty of tears, hugs, and I'm-so-proud-of-you exclamations. "I want to be the very first person that you call once you're able to," his mother sternly demanded.

Ben laughed but felt a little tear coming down his face as he gave his mother one last hug. "Of course, Mom. I love you."

Before his flight boarded, he decided he should treat himself to one last meal from civilization, which he couldn't help but feel was something like a death-row situation. He got some of his favorites: twelve pieces of hot crispy nuggets from Chick-fil-A with their famous perfectly salted waffle fries and ranch sauce for his dipping pleasure, all washed down with a venti green tea Frappuccino.

Once he arrived in Los Angeles, there was a bus to take him to the San Diego base, which would be about a three-hour drive. As he was sitting on the bus, the realization that his plans were actually happening started to hit him and fill him up with butterflies. There was a line of new recruits coming in behind him, and one of them sat down next to Ben. This man was about 6 feet tall and well built, with long blond hair and two different colored eyes—one blue and one green.

There was a moment of awkward silence while they waited for departure, and then finally Ben worked up the courage to turn to him and say, "Name is Ben," and extend his hand out to shake.

The man glanced down and returned with a very firm handshake and a gruff response of "Duane" before looking away with the air of getting a job over with as quickly as possible. Before long, a short stocky man in his late 40s announced from the front of the bus that his name was Garen and that he'd be taking roll call. "This is just like when you were in high school, so just say 'here' when I say your name."

He then picked up his clipboard and began going down the list. When he had marked everyone present, he signaled the driver to start off.

As the bus trundled out of the airport and onto the highway, a few people began talking, but most recruits were staring off into the distance. Ben was desperate for something to distract him from all of his doubts and anxieties, so he tried to get a conversation going with his quiet seatmate by bringing up random subjects until he found one that interested him.

Duane didn't respond much to the topics of fishing, music, photography, sports, or movies, but when Ben asked, "You play video games?" suddenly Duane became downright chatty. They talked the whole way after that about what games they loved or hated. And Ben made his first military friend. Even though he was a few years older than Duane, Ben had the feeling his new friend would look out for him like a big brother.

Finally, the bus pulled up to the base. Now it was now "go" time. Ben and Duane did a quick scan out the windows as they stood. It looked like a typical military setting, Ben thought. There were huge buildings and soldiers marching in unison. Every bush and tree looked perfectly trimmed, and the weed-free grass was mowed at the lowest level. All was as expected. Except, of course, it had to be pouring down rain to add to the dramatic emotions most of the men were feeling. They could see men in ponchos standing at attention with the distinctly disciplined manner that could have come only from years of practice. These men were awaiting the new recruits to give them a not-so-warm welcome to their new homes and start the process of breaking their spirits down so that they could be rebuilt anew.

CHAPTER 4

The whole bus was emptied in a matter of seconds by the large and intimidating drill instructors. In the midst of all the yelling and being rushed out to join a crowd of recruits from other busloads, Ben somehow managed to stick with his new friend Duane. When the recruits stood at attention, each instructor began yelling things such as, "You're mine now!" or "Your mamma isn't here, so time to man up!" One of the drill instructors spotted Ben and made toward him, perhaps deciding he would make a nice first victim.

But Ben managed to keep still while he felt the heat from the instructor's breath and bits of spit flying as the man screamed into Ben's face, "You are a filthy, little, tiny maggot. You're no bigger than the size of my boot! You aren't going to make it one week! Do you think you have the grit to get through this, you little pipsqueak?! DO YOU?" Ben knew already the protocol for the proper response. He had done a little research and watched videos to better prepare himself and learned that they take strong offense to being called "drill instructors" since that's an Army term. So, Ben yelled back, "Yes sir!"

After about ten minutes of this treatment, the recruits were then corralled to the next stage, which was called "recruit receiving." This is where everyone got their first haircut in which they shaved all the way down to the skin, leaving only a thin layer of hair. It was fast paced, and the men giving haircuts did not speak to them. Ben watched as Duane's long blond locks were shorn off unceremoniously to the floor. Duane was shuffled aside and sent to join the finished line of shorn men along the wall. When Ben had finished and was in line with him, Duane stood rubbing his hands over his head, his eyes glued to his hair clippings.

"Missing something?" Ben teased.

Duane merely glared.

They were then told to get their gear, which included uniforms, toiletries, and writing supplies. Ben was surprised to find that he would be able to write his family—he had heard that outside contact was forbidden during boot camp. They were then put through medical, dental, and strength tests consisting of a half-mile run, sit-ups, and pull-ups to see if they were in shape to begin basic training. Ben was very nervous during this stage since he was trying to hide his health issues, but he somehow managed to get through all the basic tests.

Week one through four consisted of strenuous physical training, martial arts, and classes to transition from civilian to recruit. His fellow recruits, especially Duane, began noticing Ben's "gangster" walk and how he was always the first one out of breath when they went running.

"Hey, man. I've been noticing issues with you. Are you okay?" Duane asked Ben one day as they were getting ready for bed after a very long day of physical activities.

"Yeah, bro, I'm fine. I've been checked out before. It's just a flare up. It'll pass."

Duane simply responded with, "Okay, bro..." and reached for his tooth-paste across the sink. But Ben could tell that he didn't believe him.

During these first few weeks of physical training, they also began learning the history of the Marine Corps and values of honor, courage, and commitment. Ben was able to comprehend everything during each class, but each following day, he found he could not remember much of it. He began to worry whether he'd even pass the tests. Ben didn't want to raise any alarms to anyone in charge, so he leaned on Duane, who acted as a true friend and helped him study.

The final phase of the first four weeks would be spent on weapon handling and completing the confidence course. Thankfully, Ben had been raised around guns and had often hunted back home.

He reminisced back to a time when he was in a blind with his father. A deer had just come out into the open, and he had reached for the gun in the dark when his dad grabbed his wrist and said, "Do not ever pick the gun up like that in the dark! You've got the barrel toward you! You have no idea if there is something wrapped around the trigger that would make it go off."

Yes, Ben assured himself as he was handed a gun by his commanding officer. *I have the benefit of having grown up with a gun safety expert.*

The next few weeks, they underwent close combat training and marksmanship practice with their issued rifles. This is when Ben began a major shift in an undesired direction. It happened while on the obstacle course one early morning. They were all running as quickly and efficiently as they could. He and Duane motivated each other throughout the course. They approached the seven-foot obstacle wall and began the climb together.

"You got this, brother!" Duane called to him after he noticed Ben was gasping for breath. He knew Duane could see the pain in his eyes, but he hoped he could also see the fight to keep pushing.

The top of the wall was finally approaching. With all his might, Ben reached one hand to the top, and as he began to force himself up the final ascent, he felt a scream rip out of his lungs, which seemed to muster the last bit of energy he had been hiding. Duane was right next to him, yelling along with him, and both of their heads began to peak over the top. Duane threw his leg over the wall first, but he mistook the distance between himself and Ben. His boot collided into the back of Ben's head, which was slammed face-first into the wall. Ben's face bounced backward, and his body followed. He fell to the ground, unconscious, as others surrounded him, including Duane, who was in complete shock.

Very slowly, Ben opened his eyes. He could see only blurs of faces at first and felt confused about what had happened. His head and neck were clamped between braces. The blur that Ben thought must have been a doctor explained that he was in the infirmary and that they were going to run some tests.

"We believe there is something going on that needs to be looked at. How are you feeling?"

"Umm...I'm feeling okay, I think. I uhm...have a headache, and I feel very nauseated."

The doctor took note of this and ordered an MRI of his full back and brain. This was to make sure his central nervous system was working properly. They also thought maybe there was something wrong with his spine.

Ben fell asleep waiting for the results and woke up later to the sound of his commanding officer asking about him. He could swivel his head now, as the brace had been removed, and he looked over to find the doctor and the officer in the doorway. The doctor declared, "Benjamin is unfit to serve with this condition, and he will be medically discharged. It is far too dangerous for him to continue." Ben watched as the officer ground his teeth, nodded solemnly, signed the proper paperwork, and left.

Ben still had no idea what was happening. Everything was hazy, and he still had a headache. He tried to sort out what had just been said, but it didn't make sense. Didn't he just have a concussion? The doctor slowly made his way to his bedside, holding what looked to be a large folder of papers and a laptop. He let out a depressed sigh as he made it to the bed and gave Ben a serious look as if *he* were the one waiting for the bad news.

"The MRI came back, son. We saw that your spinal cord was much larger than normal. It took us a bit to figure it out, but you have a rare structural defect called Arnold Chiari malformation type 1, where the cerebellum, but not the brain stem, extends into the foramen magnum, which is the opening at the base of the skull. This interferes with the flow of spinal fluid, and as pockets of fluid build up, a cyst forms. So, the large spinal cord turned out to be a spinal cyst called syringomyelia that goes from the cerebellum in your brain to the middle of your back. There are different types, and the higher the number, the more severe it is for the patient. Type 1 is the most common type of malformation and can sometimes require surgery to slow the progression of blockage. You'll have to see a specialist when you get home to determine whether you need surgery.

Ben had been staring at him in horror this whole time, unable to speak. His body was completely still, but his mind raced. All of his weird health issues...that feeling deep inside that something was wrong...The doctors who had told him he was fine...all his plans for a glorious military campaign and photography career.

"But what about basic training? Can I come back?"

"I'm sorry, Ben, but the Marine Corps cannot use you anymore, and you are to be medically discharged from service," the doctor said.

All Ben could let out was, "Thank you, doctor," before he looked away, losing the battle to hold back tears. Ben was so frustrated that he was not in control of this situation and wished they would not discharge him. That night, lying there completely alone, he did something he hadn't done in so long. He prayed a long and thoughtful prayer in tears and frustration.

"God...hey, this is your...uhm...son Ben. I am probably not your favorite, but I need your help. I am really struggling. I don't know if you can heal me, but that would be great, or just show me the plan? I don't know if there is a plan. I don't know what to do...I have been really trying here. I mean I always felt like you put me on this earth to help or inspire people, but I'm sitting here trying to figure out the plan. Yeah...so...thanks. Amen." He closed his eyes and fell back to sleep, knowing that tomorrow he would be headed back home. "It's all in God's timing and not ours," he told himself.

CHAPTER 5

Ben was now in a San Antonio hospital, waiting to see a neurosurgeon who specialized in Chiari. They had set the appointment to look at the scans and talk about the possibility of surgery. He had been so anxious that he intentionally avoided learning what all went into the process of prognosis and what to expect in different scenarios. He figured that what he would see would scare him, and he didn't want to put any extra stress on himself.

He and his mother waited for the doctor in the exam room for what felt like hours. Ben tried distracting himself by fiddling with all the things in the room. He made the jaw move on the model skull along with his words: "It's time for your anatomy lesson." His mother laughed. Then he used the bone hand to point at the backbone and cleared his throat, saying in an overdramatic professional voice, "So this is your spine. Isn't it divine?" But when he started making the legs dance, his mother, failing to suppress a grin, told him to stop playing with it before he broke it. They heard a booming voice from the hallway telling a patient to come back to see him in a few months. Ben abruptly returned the skeleton legs to their stand, returned to his seat, and stared anxiously at the door.

A very tall man with hair white as snow walked in with his laptop. He had an air about him that made Ben think he might have been raised in the countryside. The doctor's black boots took Ben back to a time of working on his family's ranch, and a memory of when he was twelve flashed in his mind.

He was on top of a calf, holding on for dear life inside the old wooden shoot that had to be close to a hundred years old. "Okay, Ben, you ready?" his father asked while standing at the other end, ready to open the door. His grandfather and uncle were standing there ready for a laugh. The gate was opened, and the calf shot out as fast as he could, trying to buck this annoying kid off. Ben was thrown off in a matter of seconds and looked over to see his family members rolling on the ground laughing.

Ben felt like that little kid now, with the doctor about to open the gate and his news about to throw him to the ground. He was forced to refocus when the doctor said in a thick country accent, "You must be Benjamin! Do you prefer Ben or Benjamin?"

"It doesn't matter to me, but be careful to not call me 'Ben' in front of this one," Ben replied, pointing to his mother.

His mother rolled her eyes and said, "Look, I named you Benjamin and not Ben, so it just bothers me. But, whatever." The doctor laughed good naturedly, said, "I'm Dr. John," and extended his hand to shake theirs.

Dr. John had a fun and relaxed demeanor, but he knew how to be serious too. Some would call it a good bedside manner. Ben and his mother felt comfortable with the doctor and connected with him despite the devastating news he was about to deliver. "Ben, I'm going to be straightforward with you...The size of your spinal cord worries me. I honestly don't know how you are able to function. This is the largest spinal cord I've ever seen in my practice.

"The cyst growing in your spinal cord is called a syringomyelia, or syrinx for short, and it was brought on by the malformation. The syrinx wreaks havoc inside a spinal cord, destroying things such as important nerves. This causes weakness, stiffness, and pain, among many other symptoms, and this is what we believe is causing the problems you are having with your leg and breathing issues. I strongly recommend surgery very soon." Dr. John went on to explain how the procedure would be done, and how long recovery should take.

He said the surgery would be a "decompression," and his relaxed and confident way of speaking seemed to indicate that the procedure was routine. He would go into the back of Ben's head, making about a three-inch incision to get to his foramen magnum and remove some of the skull to make room for his brain. He would then shave the first two vertebrae to make even more room to allow spinal fluid to flow naturally. In the spot where he would remove the bone of the foramen magnum, he would place a bovine patch to hold the brain in place and direct the spinal fluid down the spinal cord.

Just when Ben was feeling that his problems would soon be fixed, Dr. John said two things that caused his insides to jolt. "The trickiest part of the procedure is very slowly closing you back up without causing a spinal fluid leak. If it's not perfect, then I would have to go back in there to fix it. And the other thing you need to know is that this surgery is not a magical fix for everything. Some of your symptoms might go away, but some new ones might arise. There is a chance the cyst inside of your spinal cord might not even shrink after surgery, though I believe it will. My primary goal is to stop it from growing anymore and prevent the symptoms from getting worse, Ben." The doctor's voice had now taken on a deep somber tone. "Unfortunately, I don't expect it to completely go away. What you're living with right now will be with you forever."

They decided to tell the doctor that they would like a little time to think about this very big decision. Once home, they searched out friends they thought would be helpful for deciding whether to go forward with surgery. Unfortunately, they knew no one who knew anything about Chiari but found a few friends who had gone through other extensive surgeries. These friends told them that they should seek out a second opinion. But having seen the images of the enlarged spinal cord and the genuine concern of the doctor, Ben and his mother believed that he knew what he was talking about. His mother was waiting for Ben to make the decision, but they both knew what it would be.

What was holding Ben back was that going forward meant acknowledging that he would never again know what it felt like to be pain free and that he would forever wear the label of a chronic-illness patient. He would have to build up the courage to face mounting odds throughout his life.

It took three days for Ben to do this. He went for a walk in the park with his old friend Brandon, talking about life, goals, and dreams. Ben shared with him one of his dreams. "For my whole life, I have wondered what God had planned for me. I've always felt that I'm supposed to inspire others or somehow have a positive impact on their lives. I just don't know where to begin. I could really use a 'burning bush' from God telling me what to do. Life is so complicated!"

He got on the phone that afternoon and informed the doctor's office that he was ready to schedule the surgery. It was now scribbled on the calendar that hung from the fridge: January 5th. He would get to enjoy Christmas and even have a New Year's party with his family before enduring this next stage of life. Now that things were settled, his thoughts turned to Duane, who was still in basic training and had yet to hear what had happened to Ben. So, he went to his wooden desk, dug out some paper, and found his favorite pen.

Dear Duane,

Hey, brother! I was just thinking about you and felt like I should probably update you on what's happening. First off, I don't want you to think that this is your fault, bro. This is a birth defect that I had no idea I was living with, so the accident just brought it to light. It's called an Arnold Chiari malformation, and basically, what that means is my brain is falling out of my skull. They are going to perform brain surgery soon, but don't worry, man! I should be back home after two nights. I'll probably even be recovered enough to make it to your graduation, bro!! I know we have known each other only a few weeks, but I just want you to know I look to you as if you were my blood brother. Stay safe in boot camp, man. See you at graduation.

Your brother,

Benjamin

CHAPTER 6

January 5th would be a day he would remember for the rest of his life. He and his mother drove up to San Antonio the day before surgery since they lived about two hours away and were instructed to be at the hospital at 4:30 a.m. They pulled up to a large hotel, which was about a ten-minute drive from the hospital, and Ben caught sight of a steak house that was right next to it. He looked over to his mother with a grin from ear to ear. "You know...I'm not supposed to eat after midnight, and it's only 5 o'clock, Mother," he said in the most pitiful voice he could muster and with huge puppy-dog eyes. She knew that steak was his favorite meal, so she obliged to grant this final wish before the big day.

"BEEP BEEP BEEP," sounded the alarm at 4 a.m. Ben opened his eyes after about only thirty minutes of sleeping. He rolled over to turn the alarm off and fought back the urge to vomit. This whole time, he had been putting on a fake front that the thought of brain surgery was not bothering him, but truly it was eating him up. He wanted to let the anxiety out, have a breakdown perhaps. But he could tell that his mother was struggling to keep it together too. They were like two depressed clowns putting on a show for each other. They got up, quickly packed everything into the silver

Durango, and took off. Getting there as early as possible seemed the right thing to do—certainly better than waiting around in the hotel room. Ben thought absurdly of something his dad always told him: "To be early is to be on time, to be on time is to be late, and to be late is to be sorry." But Ben thought darkly to himself, "I may be sorry no matter what."

They pulled up into the parking garage of the huge hospital, and after minutes of searching, found the perfect parking spot. The butterflies multiplied in his stomach when his mother turned off the engine. They both climbed out of the car and made their way inside. They were soon overwhelmed by a maze of hallways and signs. Their pretense of calmness cracked when they were stopped by a nurse as they accidentally went into a staff-only area. His mother's eyes were tearing up as she said, "Sorry, this is our first time here, and we have no idea what we are doing!"

When the nurse saw their stricken faces, she said, "Hey, y'all are okay! It happens all the time!" She directed them to an elevator that would take them to the right floor.

Finally, they reached the correct desk, where they were greeted by a young man just a little older than Ben. Unfortunately, this was his first day on the job. He kept squinting at the computer screen and asking them for their names, the doctor's name, and other information, seemingly being unable to locate them in the system. He finally called over a more experienced person to direct him on the computer.

"Okay, here we go! You are all checked in, and here is the initial paperwork that needs to be filled out. Oh, and here is your wristband. This is going to be your identification here!" The young man insisted on helping put on this wristband that read Ben's name and much of his personal information. After this exchange, they were pointed to a waiting area nearby that had only five people. They sat down, and his mother began to fill out all the necessary info for Ben.

The people waiting were on average in their 50s, and all of them had their eyes glued to a television, which was broadcasting Fox News. One man, who had to be in his mid-60s, showed up a minute later, sipping on coffee and wearing scrubs with a tag that read, "Volunteer." As Ben discovered, his duties were simply to take the patients to the next station, but he apparently felt the need to go above and beyond. He went around and asked patients what kind of surgery they were there for and which doctor they had and listened to their concerns. He kept telling them they had the best doctor and the best hospital and that they had nothing to worry about. He occasionally liked to make light-hearted jokes. However, when he came over to Ben and asked about his doctor, he said, "Ah! Dr. John. I'm pretty sure he just finished with his last settlement."

Ben didn't know how to react to that since he wasn't sure if he was joking or not. He just gave a half smirk and looked away, but he thought to himself, "Why would anyone tell someone that right before a surgery?"

Before he could brew on it further, he heard someone call, "Benjamin?" A staff worker had arrived with a clipboard to instruct the volunteer to take Ben and his mother to one last waiting room. They sat there in silence for nearly twenty minutes, wishing the hospital would move along more quickly. The short time felt like hours, with Ben contemplating many things, including what the volunteer had said. Had the doctor really been sued for malpractice multiple times?

Finally, a nurse approached him. "Can you please tell me your date of birth?"

"July 1st, 1992."

She responded simply with a nod. Every time he spoke with a new staff member, he was asked this question, and Ben was beginning to wonder whether they were testing his cognition. He was now taken to a private room and given a robe. The nurse instructed him to take off all his clothes and put them in a huge trash-bag-like sack. "We will come back in a few minutes to put in your IV," she said. Ben's heart began to race at the thought of the soon-to-come needle piercing him, which led to the inevitable dread of the impending knife. So, to distract himself from this, he giggled at how revealing his robe was. Minutes after lying down, his mother walked in.

He couldn't face her expression of tense worry, so he obnoxiously busted out laughing, which had the desired result of changing her expression to one of confusion. "Mom, I'm *BUTT NAKED* under this blanket, and I find this absolutely hilarious!" he said in a high pitch tone.

She rolled her eyes, forced a few laughs, and responded, "You are a dork..."

A seemingly experienced nurse with short black hair walked in, asking whether she was talking to Ben and, of course, for his date of birth. "Okay, Mr. Benjamin, I am here to insert your IV for all the fluids that you will need."

He responded with, "Great...just to let you know, I am a big weenie when it comes to needles, so I'm going to stare at this beautiful picture." He indicated a framed print on the wall. She just acknowledged his statement unconcernedly, however, and began her work, just as she must had done with hundreds of other patients. He tried making casual conversation, but she didn't have much of a chatty bedside manner. Later, Ben would realize that despite her untalkative nature, he was lucky to have such an experienced nurse for this. She inserted the needle quickly into his hand, but somehow Ben still managed to have a few beads of sweat go down his back, and he tried to focus on breathing and to not faint, as he sometimes had when blood had been drawn in the past.

After the experienced nurse walked out, a very chipper one named Nicole replaced her. She seemed to be thrilled to meet Ben, as if she had been waiting all morning to do so. Then she turned around to tell his mom, "Okay, Mamma, I'm going to steal him right now, and we are going to go to the third floor. We are going on a secret elevator that only Ben and I are allowed to be on. But I'm going to need you to go down that hall, take a left, and jump on *that* elevator! We will be waiting for you in the next area."

Instead of demanding his date of birth, refreshingly, Nicole asked conversationally, "So! How old are you?"

Ben responded, "I'm twenty-three, ma'am." Grateful for the chance of a distracting and friendly conversation, he added, "How long have you been a nurse?"

CHAPTER 7

Ben had no idea that he would be rolled around from room to room the rest of the morning as if he were a king. The final destination before surgery found Ben in a large room with many cloth dividers. He looked over to see his mom texting on her phone, more than likely updating friends and family on how things were going so far. Nicole left him there in the first divided room, and though he couldn't see anything beyond the curtain, he could hear it all. There was a continuous blend of beeps, coughs, and murmuring conversations.

When he asked, "So how is dad doing?" his mother responded, "He is on his way to Burnett, Texas right now. He sure wishes he were here." Ben's father was a mobile MRI specialist, which there was a shortage of, so that unfortunately meant he was away a lot.

"What is the little brother up to?" he asked.

"He was pretty upset after we left, so Grandpa Lemke took him hog hunting to distract him."

Ben thought back to one of his own favorite memories of hunting—it was also his scariest. He and his grandfather, uncle, and father were hog hunting after a huge herd had come through and rooted up the hay field.

They had walked up on a three-hundred-pound boar and shot at it, only to have it run away with a horrendous squeal. The group believed they should never let an animal suffer, so they searched to see if in fact it had been hit. They all split up, Ben going with his uncle. The two had just approached an opening in the forest when the boar charged Ben, who just barely had time to send out the bullet from his 243 Remington youth rifle.

He had thought, as he was facing the angry eyes and tusks of the wounded animal flying at him, that it would be his last day on earth. And now, lying in the hospital bed, scared out of his wits, he hoped he would once again be proven wrong.

He and his mother sat there for nearly an hour past the scheduled surgery time and began to ask the medical staff what the holdup was. Unfortunately, no one had an answer for them, and they instead listed out reasons why the surgeon *might* be running late. It seemed no one knew where Dr. John was. Nurses periodically came in to check how they were doing and whether they needed anything.

Ben's curtain was partially left open after the last check-in, and Ben could see an elderly patient across the walkway. There were wires and tubes attached all over him, and an oxygen mask obscured half his face. He was pale as ice and seemed to be going in and out of consciousness. He reminded Ben of one of his grandfathers who passed away from liver failure. Ten-year-old Ben had walked into his grandparents' house, which smelled of alcohol and cigarettes, to find his pale-as-ice Papa, who had looked at his grandson but could not speak because of all the drugs that were given to him to make his passing as painless as possible.

Suddenly, Ben was brought back to the present when a nurse gave him the last piece of paperwork before the big surgery. Ben scanned it to find that it was an informed consent document, with all the possible surgery outcomes listed. The last item on the list was "death." Ben took a deep breath and glanced at the old man across from him.

After he signed it, his mom asked, "So, does this mean the doctor is here?"

The nurse replied, "Yes! He will come talk to y'all shortly about what's next and what to expect."

Ben and his mother both let out a sigh of relief and felt this was the time to make final mental preparations for what was to come. Little did they know that what they prepared for would be nothing they expected.

Several minutes after the nurse left, they heard a loud booming country voice and the clicking of boots. "That is definitely Dr. John coming," his mother said, laughing.

Sure enough, the doctor had finally arrived and confidently announced that this surgery would take about two to two-and-a-half hours tops unless complications arose. He added that he could see Ben staying in ICU overnight and be sent home to rest up after that. "Get back to what a 23-year-old should be doing," he added. "The anesthesiologist will soon come to administer what we call 'the cocktail.'"

Ben's mother could not contain herself as she asked him why he was so late for the surgery.

"I'm terribly sorry about that," Dr. John said. "I'm not typically late, but the Bible study I lead once a week went late today. We had a lot to cover and needed to put in some extra prayers." He hesitated for a moment, and then added, "Would it be okay if I pray over you for a moment, Ben?'

Ben smiled. "Absolutely, Doc!"

Dr. John bowed his head, and everyone followed, closing their eyes tight. Ben suddenly felt chills down his body as his doctor said a simple and quick prayer. Later on, Ben would realize that the chills were the Holy Spirit coming into him, filling him with peace for whatever outcome was to happen. God already knew what was going to happen, but Ben had no idea.

It was the last time they would wait before the surgery, and Ben's mother looked tentatively at her son for a few moments before asking in a tone that indicated she had been holding back, "Are you nervous?"

The answer would have been "yes" at any point up until this pivotal moment. Throughout his life, he had believed in God, but he had never really faced a situation where he had to truly depend on God. Some would say that he had been a "lukewarm Christian," which basically means he was stagnant in his growth with God. He had attended church almost like it was an item on a checklist of things a man of God was supposed to do.

As he was looking at his mother, for once not trying to distract them both from their fears and feeling that sense of calm that had filled him when the doctor had prayed, he knew the answer. "You know...not really, because whatever happens, God has this already planned out, and it's in his hands." Ben meant it fully in his heart, and he knew he was now finally ready for what God had planned for him. His mother was left speechless and holding back tears. His pronouncement brought so much peace to the both of them.

A very short old man pulled the curtain back quickly, and with him was a young man whose eyes looked a bit glazed over as if he hadn't had his morning coffee yet. The old man smiled genuinely. "Are you the one-and-only Mr. Benjamin?" the doctor said enthusiastically.

Ben chuckled, "Yes sir, I am."

"Please, call me Dr. Bob. This is Gary, who is shadowing me today. Since he is a student, I do have to ask if this is okay with you."

Ben nodded.

Dr. Bob went through all the protocols that come with anesthesia, and when he brought up what Ben thought was the worst part, Ben asked his first question. He shivered at the thought of a catheter and remembered some horror stories other men had told him about how painful they are. "Please tell me that I'm going to already be asleep when the catheter goes in and is taken out?"

Dr. Bob said regretfully, "Well...you're going to be asleep when we put it in, but when you wake up, you'll still have it in because your bladder takes a while to come back online. So, for your safety, it has to stay."

"Ugh!" Ben grimaced. "I understand..."

"Alright, are you ready for the initial cocktail before you get the big stuff to go to sleep?"

When Ben agreed, the doctor took a syringe from his student and counted down from three, inserting the needle into his IV. When he got to "one," Ben felt darkness creep over him, and the room began to spin. He struggled to keep his eyes open but wanted to see the operating room. He was curious whether it would look like what he had seen in movies. He heard a nurse say, "Okay, Mamma, say goodbye. We will see you in a few hours."

This whole time, his mom had been fighting back tears, but as they began to wheel Ben away, she let all the tears come at once. Ben had never seen her cry this way, and he knew he would never forget it. Even in his very drugged-up state, he called out to her as if he were a young child again, though it was a bit slurred. "It's going to be okay, Mamma. I love you!" Then he could see only the lights and the ceiling as they wheeled him out.

A moment later, Ben spoke again, this time to the man who was pushing him along. "Woah...I feel pretty darn good right now! I am going to try and stay awake to see the operating room."

The man laughed and responded, "Good luck." They entered the elevator, and Ben felt it drop before he drifted off into a deep and peaceful sleep.

CHAPTER 8

A few hours after his brief hazy awakening in which he had tried to tear away his plastic mask, Ben woke up slightly more aware. He now found the mask had been replaced with nasal oxygen tubing. Much more comfortable. But he still could not move his head, he discovered. There was a mound of pillows and towels bracing his head on all sides. The loud beeps had stopped, and the room was now deathly quiet. But he couldn't see that anything else was different from before, except that now he found his mother sitting in a big soft recliner, just at the edge of his vision, and tapping away on her phone.

"It's too quiet in here, Mom. Can you please put on music?"

She leaped up beside him and exclaimed, "Yes! What kind of music would you like me to put on?" To her surprise, Ben asked for worship music. She knew that wouldn't normally have been his first choice, but she obliged without comment.

After a few minutes of staring at the ceiling and listening to the worship music, he fell back asleep once again. He felt himself drifting in and out for several more hours until, finally, he woke up more alert and asked softly, "How'd it go?"

He could tell she was reluctant to speak of it but that she felt it was no good hiding it. The doctor had needed to do far more work than expected. The surgery lasted two more hours than planned because there was more damage and crowding at the foreman magnum, and they had found another cyst growing on the bottom of his brain. He was in critical ICU to be watched 24/7. This second cyst they found was called an arachnoid cyst, which is non-cancerous type that grows on the membrane covering the brain and spinal cord. It needed to be removed because it was dangerously large.

Removing the cyst had required cutting some of the brain as well to clear the opening for spinal fluid to flow. Unfortunately, this part of the brain was in charge of motor control, and the entire area was swollen from the surgery. Ben was stunned to learn that he was paralyzed from the neck down. And it was unclear whether this was temporary due to the swelling or whether too much brain had been removed.

It is especially unfortunate to be paralyzed after a surgery. The oxygen tube dried out his nostrils to the point of intense itchiness. And it wasn't the only place he felt itchy. Asking his mom to scratch various places on his body for him was pretty embarrassing, but it was unbearable to try ignoring them.

Doctor John arrived, his boots clacking through the doorway, for a walk-through check that evening. He began assessing Ben by running his finger on the bottom of his foot and asking him whether he could feel it. He next moved over him, testing various reflexes. Then came a test of Ben's proprioception, which is the ability to know where your body parts are. For this, the doctor grabbed each toe in succession and asked Ben which one was being touched without Ben looking.

Fear crept into his heart as he struggled to tell the doctor which toes were being touched. Every toe he said was simply a guess. The doc wrote down the notes for this examination without a word.

When he asked Ben what his pain level was, Ben answered, "Pretty low. All I can feel is itchiness right now."

"We'll be keeping you in critical ICU a little longer," Doctor John said as he turned to leave.

Ben's mother chased him out to confront him. "Why did this happen to him? Why is he paralyzed?"

"I had to remove so much that he had to be rewired in a way. All the connections that the brain uses to tell the body how to move...all of these have been changed now. He'll have to start over and relearn everything."

"Will he be able to have a normal life? Will he be able to walk again?"

"I don't think he'll *not* walk again, but I can't predict how long it will take to relearn. It really depends on him."

After two days of lying completely still, Ben started to regain some movement, but it was very spastic. He even came close to scratching an itch on his nose but ended up punching himself in the cheek. The anesthesia began wearing off and was replaced with strange and painful sensations. A consistent electrical pulse passed through his body. Nerves over-fired with every move he attempted or even at random without warning. This was the most painful thing that he had ever felt.

On the third day, a plate of hospital food arrived, and although it had smelled wonderful, the moment his mother had tilted a bite of the food onto his taste buds, he realized that it was the worst food he had ever eaten. It was a rubber version of eggs, and it ultimately ended his appetite for eggs forever. And just when he was trying to come up with a sufficient excuse as to why he shouldn't eat it, a new person arrived to see him.

It was a young woman about the same age as Ben. She had long blond hair, lovely blue-green eyes, and the whitest teeth Ben had ever seen. She said in a sweet and calm voice, "Hi, Mr. Benjamin. My name is Julia. You can call me Jules. I am an occupational therapist. Are you up to starting a little bit of therapy?"

"I am if you are," Ben replied before nodding enthusiastically to his mother in response to her asking whether she should move his food tray away.

Julia chuckled and said, "We are going to start very small. First is to train your hands to eat."

Ben groaned inwardly as his mother returned the rotating table over his lap. Julia gently grasped his hand and guided it over the silverware, maneuvering his fingers to grasp the fork. He immediately lost the grip as his hand spasmed with a jolt of pain.

Frustrated, he asked to try again only to fail once more. She then firmly held his fingers around the fork, taking full control of his hand and asked him to bring the fork to his mouth. He focused as hard as he could, only to have his arm jerk at the last second, stabbing him in the face with the fork. Julia had to control all of his movements after that in the hope that muscle memory would kick in at some point.

She came at every meal, but there didn't seem to be any progress. He began to feel discouraged. Nights were the hardest for him. When he finally had enough morphine in his system to sleep, the nurses had to wake him up for checks and little things. And every time they did, the pulses of pain shot down his body, and he would inevitably cry out in pain and beg them to push the morphine button. "It hurts so bad. It's like electricity all over my body," he would say, stretching his arms out in a futile attempt to escape the pain.

Then a nurse or his sleep-deprived mother would try to help him. They massaged his arms and legs, moved them around to encourage blood flow, and tried comforting him. But everything they tried ending up causing him more pain. There was a point during his critical-ICU stay when his nerves were so overreactive that simply touching his skin with anything, even something as soft as a feather, would start a cascade of pain that spread everywhere. So eventually, the nurses decided to not wake him up for every visit.

However, he woke up one night to find Julia praying aloud for him. He pretended to be asleep while he listened to her soft voice in the dark.

"Father God, I am praying to you today for your son Benjamin. He is such a great young man in need of your healing. God, please come over your son and show him that you are in fact with him in the fire. Speak over his heart and bring him peace. You are a loving and powerful God! I believe in my heart that you will heal this young man and that he will go out to share the wonderful news and glorify you, Father God. Thank you for blessing me with getting to know Ben and his wonderful mother. Amen."

Ben felt a wave of peace wash over him, and he wondered whether she had done this before while he had slept.

Chapter 9

After a week and a half of being in ICU, Ben was moved a step down to NICU since he was getting a little more fluid with his movements. He still could not walk or feed himself, however.

On the first day after being transferred, Julia arrived for his therapy session, bouncing on the balls of her feet and grinning from ear to ear. "Okay, Benjamin. Today, our goal is to get you to touch your nose with your pointer finger!" she exclaimed.

"You must have had plenty coffee this morning," he replied while rolling his eyes and chuckling at her hyper enthusiasm.

She brought his bed up to a sitting position and touched his right arm, instructing him, "I want you to bring this pointer finger up to your nose."

Determined to achieve this task, he slowly brought his hand up, trying not to hit himself again. He almost went cross-eyed while staring at his finger, which was coming closer and closer to his nose...only to find his finger suddenly not moving anymore. He wiggled it around, trying to figure out the problem. Then he began to laugh. "Ah, darn it! My thumb is in the way..."

Julia giggled with him and helped free up the obstruction. He then successfully touched his nose, which was a huge milestone in his progress.

They celebrated with cheers, and Ben even attempted a thumbs up, which turned out more like he was greeting a surfing buddy because his pinky stuck out too. "All right! Surf's up, dude!" was Julia's lighthearted response. "You're doing great!"

What was even more cause for celebration was the fact that he no longer felt the constant electric-like pulses going through his body. They only came around whenever he did something physical like attempting to stand up, which he realized he was nowhere close to managing.

As Ben continued therapy over the next few weeks, he still struggled with his faith but felt like God was there with him. He couldn't touch his nose without someone holding back his thumb. He didn't get any closer to feeding himself or walking. He got frustrated and even angry sometimes as he failed nearly every exercise he attempted in therapy. But then, he would imagine himself lying in the dirt. He would visualize picking himself up, dusting himself off, and continuing to push forward, swinging at every-thing the devil threw at him. Ben tried to remember that God should be praised in both good and bad times.

One afternoon, late in the second week of being in NICU, his mother was telling Ben about how their family was building a ramp on the patio for Ben to get in the house easier, when they were interrupted by another therapist, a very short and stalky Hispanic man with black and silver hair.

Although Ben had never seen him before, the man said, "Hey, amigo! How are you feeling today?"

Ben took an instant liking to him. The man, named Mario, started right away with his therapy session, telling him what his plan was for the day and asking Ben what his therapy goals were.

"I want to walk again," Ben said.

"Great. And now *my* goal for you," he grinned. "You're going to learn to dance the salsa." He demonstrated with an invisible partner.

Ben laughed. "Sure, just as soon as I can get out of this bed."

"First step is sitting up," Mario said as he helped Ben get into a sitting position, one of his strong arms across Ben's back and around his shoulder. "What we need to do is engage your core muscles and teach your brain to again have trunk control. Now, let's see if you can sit up on your own, Ben." Mario slowly released his arm from Ben.

Ben panicked for a moment. He hadn't tried this yet and didn't expect himself to be able to do it. But to his surprise, he *was* able to sit without support...for about ten seconds. Then he fell back into Mario's arm. Mario made him do it three more times.

"Looks like you need to rest now," Mario said after Ben broke out in a sweat. "You did great, and I'll see you again tomorrow."

Ben, exhausted, soon fell to sleep with a smile on his face.

That evening, he was awoken gently by his mother. "They're saying they're going to give you an MRI now to make sure everything is working and to see whether the cyst has shrunk."

Ben was moved over to a gurney and rolled down to the MRI room. This was the most movement he had experienced for two weeks, and as the gurney turned a corner, he began to feel nauseated. Sweat formed on his brow, and he felt on the verge of throwing up. He deepened his breathing in an effort to keep it at bay. He suspected the spasms of vomiting would not be good so soon after brain surgery.

After what felt like hours of being wheeled around, staring at all the lights streaking by, Ben made it to the destination. Three people prepared to move him off the gurney. "One. Two. Three," a man counted in a firm deep voice. The deep voice sounded extremely familiar to Ben, but he couldn't turn his head to see. On "three," two of the people moved

Ben's body in a nice fluid action, but the lady moving the most important part made a slight error in timing, and Ben's neck was twisted to the side, causing him to scream in agony.

"I am so sorry, Ben! Are you okay?" she cried, trembling.

"I don't know. Just—get this over with—so I can get back—and hit the morphine button," Ben gasped.

Ben then heard that familiar voice again, and a reassuring hand gently touched his arm. "Son, I'm here and am going to take care of you." Ben could see him now, as the man leaned into his field of vision. He was wearing scrubs and a surgical mask. "DAD!" Ben exclaimed.

"I wanted to surprise you and make sure you got the right MRIs done!" His father winked at the tech to show that he was teasing.

The presence of Ben's father filled him with courage, and as he was being prepared for the MRI, he was able to lie still despite the pain and fear that his neck was not okay. He tried to focus on the strange sounds of the machine. "It sounds like a rock band that's out of tune," he joked silently to himself.

They managed to move him successfully back to the gurney without twisting this time. Back in his room, he tried to be patient as they transferred him back to his bed, and as soon as the morphine hit him, he let out a sigh of relief. His father patted his shoulder, telling him he loved him and that he needed to get back on the road for his next job.

Ben could see his parents outside the room talking. He couldn't hear what they were saying but found he didn't much care at the moment. However, he did see what looked to be hope on his mother's face, and he watched as they hugged and kissed each other goodbye. His father turned back toward Ben, smiled, and gave a salute.

When his mother returned to his bedside, Ben asked, his words slurring from the effect of the drugs, "What did Dad say? Was the MRI good?"

"He said from what he saw it looked good but that you have lots of work to do."

Ben, drifting to sleep, said, "That's good," and shut his eyes.

Several hours later, after Ben had awoken, Dr John walked in with the results. "Hey, how are you coming along?"

"I've been feeling a little bit better with the pain. I don't need the morphine pump as often anymore," Ben responded, deciding not to mention the fact that he had asked his mom to hit the button three times in the last few minutes.

"That is great to hear! We'll start weaning you off then." The doctor cleared his throat and continued. "Now, first, the good news: the spinal cyst is breaking up, and your spinal cord is shrinking. Your nerves have been over-firing so much probably because of little pieces of the cyst hitting the sides of your spinal cord.

"The bad news is that we found something else on the MRI. Have you ever had joint pain or ever dislocated any parts of your body?"

"Yes, joint pain. But I never thought much about it. Never dislocated anything, but sometimes things pop. Like when giving a handshake, for example. That sometimes makes my wrist or shoulder pop."

"Well, you have a condition that is sometimes connected with the Chiari malformation. It's called Ehlers-Danlos syndrome. It is a connective tissue disorder that can affect skin, joints, and blood vessels, depending on which type that you have. It can last years or even a lifetime, with treatments being surgery, physical therapy, or just prescription drugs to manage the pain that will never completely go away. You don't need surgery now, but there is a possibility you might need joint-repair surgery or fusions in the future to help stabilize parts of your body. I strongly suggest physical therapy as a permanent treatment for EDS," the doctor concluded.

Ben was starting to feel that he would never be better. He had been thinking that if he kept trying, he would make a full recovery, but with this news, it felt like he had been knocked back down again. Ben was good at getting back up, but he was really starting to get tired.

Chapter 10

Ben found himself rolling along on a gurney again, but this time it was a journey to his new room out of intensive care. Once again, the ceiling lights began to swirl in his vision as his stomach roiled with nausea. This time, though, he could shift his head a little on his own without suffering much pain, and when he did, the swirling lights were replaced by beautiful paintings and photos on the walls.

One photograph was of a pumpjack silhouetted against a perfect balance of ground and sky. The sunset looked as if God himself had taken a paint brush, grabbed the colors blue, orange, and red, and blended them in streaks across the canvas. As the gurney passed by it, he saw in the bottom-right corner a watermark that said *Lemke Photography*. Ben thought about how photographs are never able to capture the full image of natural beauty in the same way as experiencing it in person. He tried to imagine what that sunset might have looked like for the photographer.

At last, they arrived in his new room, 303, which a nurse told him was called a suite room because of how lavishly large it was and for its beautiful view of San Antonio through three huge windows. There was a cot already prepared for a family member to use. In another corner were a comfortable-looking recliner and a wide-open bathroom that was wheelchair accessible.

When the nurses were counting down to move him to his new bed, he stiffened and lay perfectly still, remembering the MRI transfer and the excruciating pain. When he felt himself being raised, his head began to fall backward, and he saw the wall behind him. They weren't supporting his head! He knew the pain was going to come again. He braced himself, tightening his muscles as much as he could. And then, instead of his head lolling all the way back, his head was gently caught by a nurse.

She was an older female with dark brown eyes and even darker brown hair. "You didn't think I was gunna' catch you, did ya'?" she said in a thick country accent. She calmed him with a wide genuine smile as they carefully laid him down on his new bed.

No pain. Ben sighed with relief.

He got the rest of the day off from therapy and was taken off morphine. The doctor put tramadol and Tylenol codeine on his list of medications for pain relief, along with a long list of supplemental vitamins to make sure his levels stayed at a proper range.

The following morning, he and his mother were greeted by two ladies in their mid-30s, and a cart loaded with medical supplies. They explained that they were there to remove his staples, so they gently rolled him on his side and started to work.

"Will it hurt?" his mother asked them.

"It doesn't hurt at all. It's a feeling of relief getting them out," one responded.

Ben found they were right. It felt so much better to have the staples out. He had enjoyed this new feeling for only a few minutes, however, as Julia arrived to take him to therapy.

After congratulating him on leaving intensive care, she slowly transferred him over to his wheelchair by first sitting him up in the bed and then attaching him to a gate belt. Julia held tight to this support and helped scoot him along a board that formed a bridge between the bed and the wheelchair. He imagined he was on the plank of a pirate ship with the cold hospital floor as the shark-infested waters and the wheelchair as a fishing net that would catch him on the other side.

Once he was situated in the chair, Julia asked, "Do you think you can use your hands to turn the wheels?"

Ben hesitated and then said, "Well, I'll certainly give it a shot!"

He placed his hands on each wheel and pushed forward, but his hands slipped off. He tried multiple times, focusing harder each time on the muscles needed to grasp more firmly. However, it was an impossible task, and once Julia saw Ben becoming frustrated, she opted to push him to the gym herself. As they began the journey there, she started making small talk with him, asking where he was from, his age, hobbies, and interesting things he had done.

Julia was quite surprised to learn about his acting stint with Selena Gomez. Ben had a moment of cockiness about it, but it was quickly washed away by the realization that, despite his youth, he might have already hit his full potential back then. He didn't want to be worse than yesterday. People are supposed to improve themselves every day. He thought if he didn't do that, he'd be failing at life. He drooped a bit in his chair, wondering whether he had it in him to start over like this. He had been reset back to infanthood, and it appeared that it would take a long time for him to get back to where he was before, if he even could.

They arrived at the gym, which was full of people in wheelchairs moving their feet around or talking to their therapists. Ben noticed that the average age of patients was around 70, making him feel as if he were in a nursing home. He saw a smallish office-like room with glass all around it, allowing therapists to write their notes and keep a visual of the whole room.

Ben was rolled over to a separate room off to the side for occupational therapy. Once in here, they passed a series of grab bars that allowed patients to stand while holding on to them, several pieces of workout equipment, and a large door that stood open to reveal a huge bathroom that could fit 20 people. It had railings and grab bars within it too.

Finally, they arrived at a table where Julia performed a quick evaluation and then got to work on activities to train his fine and gross motor movements. These required both fingers and shoulder movements such as writing or being able to turn a steering wheel. There was also a contraption called an arm bike, which looked like bicycle peddles except that he used his hands instead of feet. After only one minute of peddling, he was already worn out.

Ben got about a three-hour rest in his room until Mario and two men just as enthusiastic as Julia arrived and stuck out their hands to shake his.

He assumed, when they got his wheelchair ready, that he was about to use the plank just as he had done with Julia, but to his surprise, they told him they were going to help him stand up off the bed and then sit down in the chair. He was excited and a bit scared about this since he had not been on his feet in weeks. They stood him up, holding tightly onto his gate belt, which was wrapped around the top of his hips. Mario moved his own leg in front of Ben's knees to keep them from buckling.

Ben immediately began to get vertigo. He started to breathe faster to fight off throwing up or fainting, but Mario told him that would do the opposite: it would raise his heart rate and make him dizzier. Gasping for air and trying to stop the room from spinning, Ben asked, "So...how much of this standing up is actually me?"

"You're doing about 30%, which is a lot better than I thought you would do!" Mario encouraged.

They managed to get Ben shuffling, but when he tried taking a step, it was overextended and in the wrong direction. The next time he tried, his leg just gave out and refused to hold his weight at all. They let him sit in the wheelchair after a minute. He felt immediate relief from the pain and fatigue, but a second later, he was grasping around for something to throw up into. Mario reacted quickly and gave him a bag, but Ben dropped it. Thankfully, Mario already had his latex gloves on to protect from what came next...

Once the room stopped spinning and the mess was cleaned up, they said it was time to go to the gym and asked him whether he was up for trying to roll himself with his hands. Ben hesitated for moment. "Well...Jules just asked me to do that, and I couldn't quite do it. But hey, I am not opposed to trying again!" Instead of getting frustrated when he failed again, he had an idea. "So, I can't walk yet, but I can sort of move my legs, so what if we put some light weights around my ankles and I just used my legs to move the wheelchair around? This could sort of be a little bit of an exercise too?"

They were reluctant at first, they said, because they thought it might develop into a crutch and slow his recovery. However, being that his goal was to get from 100% dependence to 100% independence, they decided that being able to move on his own helped him forward in that goal. Mario went to the gym and came back with one-pound weights to wrap around his ankles. Once they were on, Ben took a deep breath and tried pushing against the cold floor with his yellow socks. He couldn't get any traction, so Mario suggested they put his shoes on. Shoes! He had gone so long without them.

And just like that, Ben no longer needed someone to push him unless he was too tired. It felt wonderful to be able to do something—anything—for himself.

Once they got to the gym, he was then transferred over to a large flat cushioned table made for lying or sitting on. It even had the ability to go up and down for making it easier or harder for the patient to access it. They laid him down very gently, making sure his head was properly supported by a comfortable pillow. Then it was time to do an evaluation in which they manipulated his joints to see how well his muscles were engaging.

CHAPTER 11

Ben went through a few weeks of doing physical and occupational therapy, making small gains nearly every day. Despite this, he sometimes felt frustration and anger trying to creep into his mindset. Some days found him fighting back tears and feeling alone. And many nights, he lay in bed, asking God, "Why me? I know that I wasn't the greatest Christian, but I never did something so horrible as to warrant this punishment."

One day, when he was feeling particularly low and Jules had transferred him to his wheelchair to go to intensive therapy, he began propelling himself forward with his feet but stopped short in the doorway as something caught his attention. He had noticed a young lady walking toward the room next to him.

Ben thought she was about the same height and age as him. She had long brown hair curtained around a small face, the cutest little nose, and hazel eyes. There was oxygen tubing going to her nose, and she was dragging a wheeled oxygen tank behind her. She also had a golden retriever by her side that was wearing a service-dog vest. She coughed, and the dog immediately looked up at her to make sure she was okay.

Ben was so taken aback by her that he barely noticed as Jules, who had not been expecting him to stop so suddenly, bumped into the back of his chair. He knew he didn't believe in love at first sight—not after living most of his life facing rejection after rejection and infatuations with every pretty girl who crossed his path. But this was different because he wasn't just seeing a beautiful woman. He was seeing a woman who radiated light as if she were an angel. He could not work up the courage to say anything, and when she had disappeared into her room, he turned his chair toward the elevator and rolled away. He was filled with instant regret.

When he and Jules made it to them gym and he was situated on the arm bike, his thoughts were only about his new neighbor. Jules noticed his inattention and must have also seen what had stopped him in the doorway earlier because she said in a knowing voice, "Something on your mind?"

He felt his cheeks redden. "Ohhhh...nothing!"

Her eyebrows rose in challenge, and Ben decided to spill the beans. "That woman who was going into the room next to mine...do you know her name?"

"Can't tell you. HIPPA privacy laws. But they don't stop you from just asking her yourself!"

These words frequently revisited his head over the next few days, and he had more time to brew on them because visits from his mother were becoming fewer and shorter than they had been right after surgery. This was because the business she had opened a few years ago was really starting to grow, and after having taken off for so long, she had a huge pile of orders for her hand-stamped jewelry to catch up on. His father tried to visit as much as he could between work trips, but it wasn't often. With his medical background, he loved to assist in his son's therapy.

"Now I want you to do the peace sign with your right hand," he once told Ben, who was doubtful but tried anyway.

He lifted his spastic arm and stared at his hand. He concentrated and slowly formed a very funky looking peace sign. He thought it looked more like a claw. "Well, there you go. It's not very good, but it's something."

His father laughed. "Look at your other hand, son!"

Ben looked down to see his left hand, which formed into a perfect peace sign. He hadn't even realized he was doing that. He stared in awe.

"Your left hand remembers how to do it. And the rest will catch up fast. You'll see."

Occasionally, friends and other family stopped by to visit him, only to leave troubled by what they saw. It was written on all their faces. They feared he might never come back from the state he was in. Despite all those fears, they all told him that they felt inspired by his attitude and smile.

One day, he had an unexpected visitor. It was his old buddy Duane from boot camp. "Wow! Dude...it is so great to see you, my bro!" Ben exclaimed. "I would uhm...get up to shake your hand, but I can't yet."

Duane didn't talk about anything that had to do with Ben's health. Instead, they sat there for a few hours talking about video games, just as they had the first time they met. He also mentioned his graduation and his new station in Washington state. There was a bit of awkward silence for a moment when Ben realized they were both thinking about the fact that Ben would never graduate from boot camp or be assigned a station.

Ben broke it with, "Hey, are you hungry? The cafeteria has pretty great food..." He stuck out his tongue to show he was being sarcastic.

Duane laughed and agreed heartily to having lunch with him.

Ben hit the call button to ask for help. A few minutes later, while two nurses shifted him to the wheelchair and helped him put on his shoes, Duane stood back awkwardly, looking emotional at the feebleness of his friend.

Ben decided to show him that he wasn't all feeble, and he pedaled his feet as quickly as he could, Duane smiling after him.

"I got your letter, and I really appreciated it!" Duane told him as they waited for the elevator. Ben looked down at the floor with a sigh. "Yeah...I don't think that I'll be able to make it to your graduation now."

Duane quickly went into recovery mode to make his friend feel better. "Hey! It's all good man, honestly. I hear they are really boring! But I'll get it recorded so you can watch it, my brother."

Ben looked back up at him and smiled. "I'd like that." They continued on their little journey, down the elevator and through a few hallways, talking about fun memories. Of course, they talked about video games too, and it was so good to just talk about something fun with his old buddy that Ben didn't even think about his paralyzed hands and being unable to use game controllers.

Once they got to the cafeteria, Ben spotted the angelic girl again with her pup beside her. He felt his heart start racing. It seemed his senses were heightened as well. The smell of the chicken spaghetti being served was suddenly stronger. He tried to not be obvious about his attention on the girl by forcing himself to scan around the rest of the room. There were patients, as well as nurses and security officers on their lunch breaks. But as Ben and Duane moved across to the ordering area on the left, Duane noticed how Ben's eyes kept glancing toward the right side of the room where she sat among many of the patrons and how he had slowed to a snail's pace. Finally, he asked, "Is there someone in here that I need to beat up or something?"

"Do you see that girl over there with the golden retriever?" Ben whispered.

"Uhh...yeah, I do," Duane whispered back, mystified.

"I'm gonna' marry her."

Duane laughed and turned back to Ben, only to discover by his expression that he was not joking. "So...does she know this yet?"

"No," Ben responded.

"Do you even know her name?"

"No." Duane's face showed astonishment. "Well...are you gonna' scoot over there, or am I gonna' have to push you over there myself?"

After a few minutes of arguing over whether they were going or not, Ben finally agreed to approach her. They got a tray of food for Ben (Duane took one look at the hospital food and decided he wasn't hungry) and made their way over to her.

Ben was fearful of rejection or to be thought of as weird, but he was a tad more confident than he would have otherwise been since he had a "wingman" to help. As Ben rolled over with Duane at his side, his heart was beating so loud that he could swear it was about to jump out of his chest. When they got to her, she looked up and smiled at them.

Duane introduced them, describing Ben as the "nicest guy he knew," and when *she* spoke, Ben thought hers was the most beautiful voice he had ever heard. "My name is Penelope, but you can call me Penny. And this is my best friend, Duke," she said, pointing at the golden retriever.

Duane set down Ben's tray at the edge of the table where Ben could roll up to it. "Well, my job is done..." He nudged the side of Ben's wheelchair, but Ben seemed frozen in place. "Alright, bro, I need to catch a ride to my friend's house."

There was a delay, but Ben finally turned to him, his eyes slightly glazed, and said, "Okay, man. I'll see you around." He smiled gratefully.

Duane just patted his friend's shoulder in response. "Penelope, it was a pleasure meeting you!" he said as he walked away, glancing back one more time to see if they were talking. "Just call me Cupid," he chuckled to himself as he left the cafeteria.

CHAPTER 12

Ben and Penny hit it off right away, talking about their lives, passions, and hopes over chicken spaghetti. In getting caught up with meeting Penny, Ben had completely forgotten that he was going to recruit help from a staff member to eat. He looked down briefly at his food as Penny was talking about her love of life. While she used her hands as people often do when talking and eating, Ben kept his arms tight under the table.

After a while, Penny connected the dots. "I could help you eat if you'd like." When she saw his expression, a mixture of shock and embarrassment, she added, "I'm sorry. I didn't mean to offend you."

"No, no...It's all okay. It just took me by surprise."

When he didn't say anything else, Penny gestured to the fork, and Ben bit his lip, wanting to say "no," but his stomach had been yelling at him for the past hour. He would just have to let go of his pride and say "yes." However, all that could come out was a head nod.

She picked up his fork and began feeding him in quiet patience. After a while, she remarked, "I can't help but feel I've met you before."

Ben said with a wink, "You might recognize me from a movie with Selena Gomez a few years ago."

Her eyes widened, then she laughed and responded, "You mean the one where you were her on-screen boyfriend and ya'll lived happily ever after?"

He nodded.

"Yeah, I haven't seen it."

He rolled his eyes, and they both laughed. They talked for hours, but for some reason, neither one of them wanted to discuss the reasons why they were being "imprisoned" in the hospital. Not yet at least.

"So, I have a little confession..." Ben said, as the cafeteria was emptying, and workers were wiping down the tables. "I saw you yesterday walking into room 302, which is right next to mine. I chickened out in speaking to you then, but I'm so glad we got to talk today." He was half grinning, half apologetic, hoping he didn't come off as weird or with a "stalker vibe."

She had a bit of a confused face for a moment but responded, "Yeah, that's my room."

"Well, then. We are neighbors!"

She laughed and said, "If you need to borrow some sugar, come on by."

"Can I *walk* you back to your room?" he said, gesturing to his wheelchair and expecting her to laugh. But he didn't expect her to laugh so hard that it would put her into a wretched hacking coughing fit. She bent over double and had an arm at the back of Duke's neck. Duke stood up and was looking up into her face as if waiting for something.

"Are you okay?" Ben asked softly when she could finally speak again.

"Yes, this is normal," she said, staring at the floor.

They made their way back to the third floor in silence, both wanting to talk about their health issues but neither wanting to scare the other person off or ruin the moment of cheer.

Once they arrived at his room, she bent down to give him a hug, and they began to part ways until she turned back and said, "Hey, Ben, I kind of have a decorated room. Would you like to see it?"

"Absolutely!" Ben exclaimed, shuffling his feet to turn the wheelchair around. When she waved for him to go ahead of her through her doorway, he refused, saying, "Ladies first!"

She smiled and stepped through with Duke, and Ben followed. Ben was speechless at what he found—instead of a hospital room, it was a beautiful bedroom. There were purple drapes on the windows with decorative strings hanging from the top. On one wall, big letters read "Faith is Love," and below were snapshots from a modern instant-print cameras, showing off countless memories of her and her friends.

On another wall were the words "Fear is a Liar," and below it was a set of Bible verses that gave encouragement. One in particular caught his eye: *Jeremiah 29:11 "For I know the plans I have for you," declares the Lord, "plans to prosper you and not harm you, plans to give you hope and a future."*

And last, on the wall next to the door, was a list of people to pray for with the title above it saying, "Warriors in battle."

Penny watched Ben studying the names of each person and what they were battling. "Most of those are friends I've gained over the years in the hospital. A lot of them are still here. I visit them when my health allows it..."

Slowly, he turned his wheelchair around and looked deep into her hazel eyes. He took a deep breath and said quietly, "Can I ask you why you are in the hospital?"

She sat down on her bed, settling Duke into his own little comfortable bed next to her, and began a long story about how she had cystic fibrosis and that it was a defective gene that causes a thick, sticky buildup of mucus in the lungs, pancreas, and other organs. The mucus in the lungs clogs the airways, trapping bacteria and leading to infections, extensive lung damage, and eventually, respiratory failure.

"The average lifespan of a CF patient is 40 years, but some of us are blessed to live longer," she concluded in a somber voice.

Ben was stunned. Her fight had been going on a long time.

She continued, "I figured that if I was going to spend most of my time here, I might as well make it more like home! Hospital rooms can be so depressing sometimes...Oh, I left out something important...I'm actually here now because I got a bad cold, which is not good for CF. Since I'm a regular here, they made this room permanent for me. I'm uhm...waiting for a lung transplant because these crappy airbags are only 30% functioning." Despite her dark pronouncement, her voice was upbeat.

Her story got even darker when she elaborated that a lung transplant had a chance of extending her life but that it would be like trading one problem for another. Her new lungs would not have CF, but the odds of her surviving the transplant would be slim. Her body could reject the new lungs, or she could have other fatal complications. It was a risk most cystic fibrosis warriors were willing to take to live a longer life. "The new lungs might last only five to eight years before you need another transplant. If you're lucky and stay active in the gym exercising your new lungs, they could last about 10 years.

"I kind of have an unpredictable schedule with my illness. Friends and family like to come visit at random times because they know things are uncertain with me. And I have to have tests done a lot. It's super depressing sometimes. But I like to sneak out and do things that make me happy like visiting friends or even leaving the hospital when I can. So, if you come visit me, I might not be in my room." She paused. "Can you tell me about your story now?"

Ben explained all about Chiari and EDS and how he had woken up paralyzed after his surgery, that he was labeled a quadriplegic, and that he would likely not have a normal life. "And when people told me that, all

I could think about was that I had lost all my purpose. You see, I always thought God's plan was for me to help or inspire people. First, I thought I could do that by being an actor. Then that fell through, and I thought a combat photographer was what I was supposed to be doing. And now I don't know what I'm supposed to do."

Penelope looked thoughtfully at him. "Did you ever think that maybe what's happening now *is* part of that plan? That you'll get through this and then inspire others *because* you went through it?"

While Ben contemplated this perspective, Penelope told Ben that she knew the hospital like the back of her hand. She offered to show him all her favorite spots and introduce him to some of her friends, and he agreed happily.

"We'll start tomorrow then. Is that alright?" Penny asked.

Ben agreed, and they parted ways. A few minutes later, both were in their own beds, thinking about each other.

The follow morning, Jules found Ben still asleep, and she gently nudged him to wake up. Once his eyes opened, she listened as he began to fill her in on everything that had happened yesterday.

"I'm so happy for you!" She patted him on the back. "Now, can you try to put your shoes on today?" At his nod, Jules handed one of his shoes to him, which was unlaced and ready to go on his foot, and quietly encouraged him, saying, "You got this."

Ben took a deep breath to prepare himself for what he knew would be quite a challenge. Grunting for a few minutes through the strain and struggle of coordinating the necessary movements, he finally slipped a shoe onto one of his feet. Gasping for air, he looked up to Jules as if to say, "There, I'm finished."

He let out a loud sigh when she said, "And I know you'll do just as well on the other one!" as she handed him the other shoe. He rested for a few minutes to catch his breath and then started again. After he had it on too, Ben was exhausted but grateful that Jules had pushed him and encouraged him to finish without seeming to feel sorry for him. He did not need sympathy right now, but he found her empathy and patience for his struggles comforting. She tied his shoes for him, transferred him to the wheelchair, and led the way to the gym.

Once there, she had him try some muscle movements that he had been unable to do in the past. But unlike with the shoes, he couldn't do them no matter how hard he tried or how encouraging she was. He knew he was having to relearn everything, and he tried to tell himself that he was being completely rebuilt by God, but he had thought he should be making progress every day. But the fact was that he wasn't even making much progress every week, and now he found it difficult to see himself getting to the next part of this new plan of God's. *Was it a new plan though? Or had God planned all this out from the very beginning?*

CHAPTER 13

He felt doubt and bitterness overcoming his mind that afternoon as he was resting back in his room. The morning's therapy had seemed pointless. The only thing he had to show for it was exhaustion and more pain. After several hours of wallowing in frustration and anger, there was a knock at the door. He quickly wiped his tear-streaked face with his blanket.

Penelope was there smiling with Duke beside her. Ben had forgotten they had agreed to meet today, but he waved her in, clearing his throat so that it wouldn't sound like he'd been crying. Duke put his front paws up on the bed and waited for Ben to pet him. Ben patted the top of the dog's head and looked up at Penny, who was hefting a bag in one hand and pulling along her oxygen tank with the other.

"I got you something!" she said by way of greeting.

"Oh, you didn't need to do that," he said, shocked.

"It's really nothing at all!" she responded with a smile. What she brought out of the bag was a roll of tape and a bunch of large strips of paper. On each strip was written a different encouraging scripture. "I could tell you liked my scripture wall, so I made these for you."

He couldn't help it: he broke down crying again. "Sorry," he murmured as tears coursed down his cheeks. "I just don't know if I'll ever get out of this chair or even brush my own teeth again."

If she was surprised by his reaction to her gift, she didn't show it. She waited until he gained control of himself and then said, "Life is so very hard. It's like it's throwing punches at us constantly, and we're dodging them. But sooner or later, it'll land a punch on us, like when we drop our defenses once things start to feel comfortable.

"But when we have been knocked flat on our backs in a deep pit of despair, we are left with two choices: one leads to crippling fear, and the other provides enough faith to let us crawl out of the pit. All we need to get started is faith the size of a mustard seed. When we can't run, we must walk. When we can't walk, we must crawl. But whatever we do, we can't give up.

"It's our job to choose faith over fear despite all the things stacked up against us. God has a plan for all of this, and if we give up on this, we are essentially giving up on *him*."

Ben stared at her in awe. He wasn't sure whether her level of positivity under her own terrible suffering constituted insanity or perfect faith, but he felt he must try harder to get out of the chair...for her...to prove she was right.

She helped him stick the chosen pieces of scripture all over his walls while he pointed where to put them from his bed. Then they got Ben transferred to the wheelchair. They were going on what she called "an adventure of a lifetime."

"I have spent much of my life here, and I know all the secret spots and some awesome tricks, like how to access the secret hospital menu, sneak in a gaming system, and get on the fastest internet," she told him as she sat down in her own wheelchair.

"I didn't know you had a wheelchair too," he said, surprised.

Her hands went to her hips, and her expression hardened. "We are going to cover a lot of ground today, and I can't walk long distances with-out...well...dying," she said sternly, pointing toward her lungs.

"Oh my gosh, I'm sorry. I wasn't like judging or anything," he said, waving his hands in front of him.

"Ha! I'm just messing with you. Have some fun with your illness. What else can you do with it?"

He broke into a grin and joined her in laughter—a wild raucous laughter that had no place in a hospital. They rolled down the hallway, and Ben paid almost no attention to what was around them—there was only her: her shining face that looked healthier somehow, her giggling that filled the hallway, her giddiness that filled him.

Halfway to the elevator, Penny covered her mouth and made a noise that sounded like crackling static before announcing, "Welcome, ladies and gentlemen, on your flight of the sick-kid club where the sights are absolutely jaw dropping and unforgettable. Please keep your hands inside the seats at all times. There will be no concessions on this flight...so have fun being hungry!" She began laughing so hard that it triggered a coughing fit. "Ouch," she said but looked forward with determination.

Ben was torn between amusement at her antics and concern over her coughs she had said were normal. "So, what's the first stop, Captain?"

"Ah, it's my secret treehouse. Or as close to it as I've ever had." They soon rolled up to an unmarked door that was placed in an odd spot in the hallway. Looking him dead in the eye, she said in a low and serious tone, "Are you ready for the coolest thing ever?"

He slowly nodded, unsure of what was about to happen and in a kind of shock at having met someone as silly (or maybe even sillier) than himself.

He didn't know how to act with someone like this, and it didn't help that he was attracted to her as well.

"There's the rope ladder," she said, indicating that he should push the handicap button to open the door, which was closest to him.

"I'm not sure I'll be able to do that," Ben said, looking down at his hands doubtfully. They were resting in a strange, twisted position in his lap.

"At least try. If you fail, it's not the end."

"Okay, but if I can't hit a huge button, I'm going to feel like I've hit rock bottom." *Especially in front of you*, his mind added silently.

"Rock bottom can be awesome!" she exclaimed. "It's the coolest opportunity for us. It's only then that we have the chance to make a whole new foundation to build our faith on! There is a purpose for hitting rock bottom, and for some, it can be easy for them to discover why. Others might not ever find it because they are stuck in the 'why me' questions. But if we can stop asking that and look around, we can see the purpose. And God is with us in every moment, rooting us on."

He nodded at her in awe once again. Then he turned and focused on the handicap button. With all his might, he began to reach his left hand up to the button. He grunted in pain and was fighting his muscles that were trying to pull against his movement. He missed the first time, having his fingers all jumbled up in half a fist, but he wasn't going to give up. Ben tried once more and connected with the button, applying just enough pressure to make the door open for them.

The opening revealed a long hallway lit by sunlight coming through several big windows. Penny led the way in, and Ben followed, pausing with a gasp at the first window. They were overlooking a large garden. There were two giant trees shading over elaborately carved stone benches. Bright flowers of all hues grew everywhere. He sat there for nearly 15 minutes, speechlessly admiring all the beauty, and Penelope admired along with him.

"What is that place?" he finally asked in a reverent whisper.

"It's the prayer garden," she said. "Let's go down to it."

So, they headed back the way they had come and were waiting at the elevator when its doors opened, and Julia stepped out.

Ben's heart sank. "Time for occupational therapy?"

"Yep! Are you bringing a friend this time?" She winked at Ben, indicating Penny.

"Oh, I'd love to come if that's okay!" Penny exclaimed.

Ben hesitated but agreed when he looked at Penny. Perhaps her support would drive him forward. He wanted to try.

CHAPTER 14

Once they got to the gym, Jules had him working on a simple child's puzzle, and once he finished it, she put shaving cream on a small table in front of him and had him write his name with it. Finally, he was using the arm bike again, and although he was feeling worn out, Penny cheered him on, and he kept going. Most significant was that he managed to sit upright without support for the entire duration with only one instance of falling over, in which Jules was there to catch him.

At that exact moment, something caught his eye at the front of the room. Someone was coming in the doorway. He recognized who it was immediately: his old school buddy, Brandon. "Hey!" Ben called to him.

His oldest friend dashed to his side. "Can I help in any way?" he asked. He held his arms out as if to catch Ben should he fall sideways again.

Ben noticed his way of speaking had become more confident after serving in the military.

Jules smiled and responded kindly, "No, it's okay. I've got him."

Ben and Brandon nodded at each other, but Ben was a bit too preoccupied to really visit. So, he simply said, "One second, man."

This prompted Penny to introduce herself and "entertain" his friend while Ben finished his therapy.

As everything was being cleaned up, Ben took a minute to reflect on everything that had happened in the past twenty-three days. The fear, the pain, the hope, the discouragement, the loneliness, his recent breakdown, and Penny's words. Maybe seeing his oldest friend had sparked this introspection. The idea of choosing faith over fear was going through his head over and over again. But he couldn't quite get there. *What is holding me back?* he asked himself.

All of a sudden, there was an explosion of feelings welling up within him. For a moment, he couldn't understand what the emotions were saying. But he realized what they *weren't* saying: he didn't pity himself anymore. He felt a voice come upon his heart, and he knew it was the voice of God.

It is time to start walking again.

He suddenly understood so much. All this time, he had felt like God had not been paying attention to him…that he had been alone in his efforts and despair. And when he had prayed, lying in the hospital bed, he had heard back, "Not right now," which he hadn't been able to accept.

The thing was that he had not been truly looking to God because all he could see was self-pity. He essentially had been wearing blinders against God, who had been jumping up and down, trying to let Benjamin know that he was right there and to trust him. God had always pursued Ben, even when Ben was not looking toward God.

But now, just as Penny had said, things looked pretty good from rock bottom. He could see better than ever. And now he understood the message and meaning. He felt a layer of trust being laid down on the foundation.

He looked Jules straight in the face and said, "I don't know how to explain this, but I'm supposed to walk now."

Her eyebrows rose up into her hairline, and her mouth came open at his proclamation. But because she had believed in Ben from the beginning, she soon broke into a huge smile and cried, "Okay, let's go!"

Ben was amazed in her faith in him. Not because he doubted what he said, but because he knew it seemed impossible from the outside. He was a quadriplegic who had lost nearly thirty pounds and had made very few improvements over the past weeks. He thought that the devil could have easily filled her with doubt, as he had been doing to Ben.

Instead, she was bouncing on the balls of her feet. She couldn't stop grinning. She turned to call for an assistant, but Brandon volunteered to help, and she instructed him to stand behind Ben and be ready to catch him in the wheelchair.

Jules wrapped one-pound weights around Ben's ankles to minimize spasticity. Then she helped him come to a stand. His body was beginning to spasm, he could feel it, but he could also feel those words inside him again.

It's time.

Penny was whooping next to him. Brandon stood amazed behind him. And when Jules let go of Ben, he was standing! He was standing all by himself!

Jules said to Ben, "While we are walking, I want you to hold onto my forearms." She extended both her arms out to him. Ben grabbed a hold and felt secure and right.

It seemed the devil was not finished with him yet though. Ben looked down at his legs and felt doubt trickling back in. But he knew the devil was trying doubly hard because Ben was so close to beginning to fulfill God's plan.

He could see now how it all had been playing out. He imagined himself as up to now having been wrestling with God in the dirt and mud. He had been trying to pin God down, screaming at him in anger and frustration and demanding answers. He had probably even thrown a few punches toward God but had never landed them. All the while, the devil had been whispering in Ben's ear, telling him that he was in this situation because of God...that God had abandoned him. But Ben knew now that he could only get the answers by trusting God. He placed down another layer of trust and concentrated on his right leg.

He took his first step in twenty-three days. Then he took another and another, looking over to Penny who was smiling from ear to ear with tears flowing down her cheeks. He took another step. And two more. He was gasping for air now, and he heard Jules say, "Ben, I just want to remind you the wheelchair is right behind you in case you need it!"

By this time, they had made it to the hallway. Ben slowly turned his head around and looked at the wheelchair. How inviting it appeared. Brandon appeared eager to catch him too. He felt his muscles ready to give in to the welcome rest. All the pain and exhaustion would feel better if he sat now. But something held him back. He had a feeling that if he gave up now, it would be harder to get up next time. Maybe even impossible. He stared at the padded seat, trying to sort out the two voices. One was the devil, and one was God.

There were two highly valuable lessons he learned that day, which would serve a greater purpose later in his life. The first was that all pain is a temporary thing and does not need to control our actions. Pain has a purpose, but it isn't to inspire inaction. The second lesson was that no matter what we have done in the past, God will forgive us. We can kick and yell at God in anger, and he will continue to pursue us. If God were not forgiving, Ben would not be walking down this hallway. It was a true miracle, he realized, and it would forever change his relationship with God.

He kept walking...down the hallway and to the elevator. Jules, Brandon, and Penny were cheering him on. A few other health workers heard the commotion and joined what now felt like a parade. He was shaking all over, sweating from head to toe, and in excruciating pain, but he made it all the way back to his room, where he collapsed into his bed. The crowd gave one last cry of triumph for him before he smiled at them, closed his eyes, and immediately fell into a deep sleep, knowing that everything had changed.

After about an hour of rest, he was awoken by Brandon and Penny talking. But as he began to stir, their voices hushed. He slowly opened his eyes and heard Penny say to Brandon, "I'm going to go do some treatments. I'll let you two catch up!" She gave Brandon a quick hug and left the room.

Brandon sat on the bed. "Long time no see," he said calmly.

Ben lifted his hands up slowly to give him a fist bump. He and Ben then began telling each other stories and reliving memories.

Finally, Brandon couldn't hold it in anymore. "So, Penny. Nice girl..." he said awkwardly, hoping Ben would spill the beans about her.

Ben was not sure what to say, but his blushing face told Brandon everything he needed to know.

Brandon grinned and stretched. "Well, I think you promised me that I'd be your best man at your wedding!"

Ben let out a silly and awkward laugh. And although he was slightly enjoying this conversation, he decided to change the subject. "I remember. Hey, have you seen the new Star Wars movie?"

Brandon had to leave soon after that to catch his plane back home. He was only on a short leave from the military after hearing about what happened to Ben. As he was leaving, he hesitated in the doorway and turned back. "Hey, I shouldn't have told you how awesome it is being in the military. Then maybe this wouldn't have happened."

"No, it's not your fault. This rare brain disorder was there when I was a kid. Remember all the problems I had? Joining the military probably helped find the source sooner is all, so don't blame yourself."

"Okay," Brandon said. "I'm sorry you're having such a rough time. But I know you're going to get through it. You were so awesome today!"

CHAPTER 15

The next day, Penelope rolled into his room, excited about showing him more of her favorite places in the hospital. "You ready to go, Benny?" she asked, uncertain whether he would appreciate her nickname for him.

He smiled and looked at her. The sun was pouring onto her face so that her eyes glistened and appeared to change to the color of honey. Other features of her face that he had not previously noticed were lit up. Her cheekbones were high and distinct, and she had a small scar on her forehead.

Her expression began to show embarrassment, and she said, "Is it okay to call you that?"

Ben realized that, instead of responding, he had simply been staring at her in admiration for a full twenty seconds. He grinned apologetically and exclaimed, "Oh, yeah! That's fine. And yes, I'm ready to go. But I don't think I should try walking today. I have the feeling I should rest for a few days. Let me just call for help to get into my chair."

Once settled in his wheelchair, he followed Penny down a series of hallways until they came to a wood-paneled wall with gold cursive letters reading, "*For with God, nothing shall be impossible. Luke 1:37.*" There was an extravagantly engraved door with long iron handles. Right above the door was a simple black sign with white letters that read, "Chapel."

"First stop," said Penny.

She stood up to open the door and moved aside to allow Ben to roll through and into the chapel.

"*I* should be opening the door for *you*," Ben said. "Maybe you think I'm old-fashioned, but that's how I was raised."

She just laughed and told him she was happy to be opening the door for him. "I'll make you a deal. You can open the door for me once you're out of the chair for good!"

Penelope decided to ditch her wheelchair out in the hallway since she knew they wouldn't be long. Once they were both inside, Ben looked around. The chapel was small—the pews could sit only about fifteen people, and here in the back seemed to be the only place a person in a wheelchair could sit. In the front of the chapel was a small table with a Bible on a riser. There were three sections of stained glass, together forming an image of a cross with the sun behind it. Ben interpreted it as representing the light God provides.

Ben whispered, "I never knew that there could be so much beauty here. I just thought of a hospital as a cold and dull place that holds a bunch of sick people."

Penny nodded in understanding. "Too often, we focus on the negatives so much that we miss the beauty in things. We've got to slow down once in a while and appreciate the small things! To stop taking things for granted is a big lesson I've learned through my many years of being in and out of this hospital." They sat in silence for a few minutes, simply appreciating the room.

At last, Penny broke their quiet contemplation. "Alright! It's time to go visit one of my very good friends. I have been wanting to tell you about her for a while. She has Chiari just like you but has some different things going on. Her name is Haleigh, and she has a sister named Avee. Hopefully, Avee is visiting because it would be so much fun to introduce you to both of them."

Benjamin was intrigued to meet someone with the same condition as him. *Would she be of similar age? Would she be able to walk?*

They got to room 337, which was on the same floor that Penelope and Benjamin were staying. Penny poked her head in the room first to check that it was a good time to visit. "Okay!" she called to Benjamin to follow her in.

"I'd like you all to meet my friend Benny," he heard her say.

Ben slowly rolled in to see a small girl of perhaps 12 sitting up in bed. She wore a neck brace that shimmered pink, and there was a feeding tube running through her left nostril and taped to her cheek. She had blond hair and blue eyes, and when she smiled at Ben, he could see that she had been through so much but that she was a fighter.

Next to her was a cot on which sat a middle-aged woman. She stood to greet Ben. "Hi! My name is Krissy, and this is Haleigh!" She indicated the girl in the bed and then pointed at a smaller girl who was sitting in a big comfy-looking chair and wearing a neck brace that was glittery purple. "That's my sweet Avee. I'm their mother." The two girls were nearly identical except that Haleigh appeared a few years older.

Ben smiled at them. "It's so nice to meet y'all!"

Avee exclaimed, "Oh, my goodness! It's Benny and Penny! You guys go together!"

Everyone laughed.

Ben noticed Penny's cheeks flushing a bit and hoped she felt the butterflies that he did at being told they "go together."

Ben and Penny stayed for what felt like hours, sharing stories of their experiences. Ben listened as the two girls and their mother took turns explaining the children's conditions. They were both diagnosed with vascular Ehlers-Danlos syndrome (in which the body does not produce enough collagen), Chiari type 1.5, tethered cord syndrome (which is where the bottom of the spinal cord attaches itself to the spinal canal), neurogenic bladder, dysautonomia (which can affect the functions of things like the heart, lungs, digestion, and sweat glands), craniocervical instability, retroflexed odontoid (in which the top joint of the spine bends into the brain), osteoporosis, hypothyroidism, asthma, food allergies, and immunodeficiency.

Ben's jaw hit the ground. It was so heartbreaking to hear what they had been through, but the courage they showed in facing each obstacle inspired him. He was reminded of a valuable lesson: there is always someone worse off than you are, and there is always something to be thankful for in any situation

CHAPTER 16

Several weeks later, Ben was sitting up in bed, watching some TV after both physical and occupational therapies. He had made more gains in both sessions, including walking longer and tracing a picture of a cat and horse. Admittedly, his tracing looked like something a three-year-old had drawn, but the progress was enough to fill him with a sense of contentment.

The TV was presenting a show about home renovation. While Ben watched three people destroying a wall with sledgehammers, he heard his door slide open. He turned to see Penelope and Duke. When his eyes met hers, he knew they weren't going adventuring.

The past few weeks, she had taken him to several more special places in the hospital, and they had visited Haleigh and Avee many times, but they had yet to visit the prayer garden. Ben had the feeling she was saving it for a special occasion. During the last few outings, Ben had noticed that her shoulders had begun to hunch forward, and the coughing fits came more often.

Today, she was hunching more severely and struggling to catch her breath, but her eyes were alight with joy at seeing him. It was obvious to them by now that they had very strong feelings for each other. Neither had said anything, but they both knew. Other people seemed to have caught on as well. A few days before, Ben had overheard a nurse refer to them as "love birds." Haleigh and her sister Avee broke out singing, "Benny and Penny sitting in a tree, k-i-s-s-i-n-g," when Ben had gently laid a hand on Penny's shoulder. The girls' mother had tried to hush them but had smirked knowingly.

Ben watched her as she sat down in the recliner next to him and gasped for breath with Duke setting his head on her lap looking worried. Ben noticed she had something hidden in one of her hands, which she tucked behind her. He waited until she had caught her breath and then said, "I've been thinking about something, and it might sound a little crazy, but don't laugh."

She stuck her pinky out toward him. "I pinky promise not to laugh."

He grinned, and though he felt foolish, he reached toward her hand. It took him several minutes to negotiate his pinky finger to meet and wrap around hers.

She smiled and brought their joined hands up and down several times before pulling back to look expectantly at him.

"You know how I have always believed that I was put on this earth to inspire others, but I could never figure out how I was supposed to do it? I had no idea where to even begin. I prayed continuously for God to give me a sign or to just help guide me down that path. Now I think that this all happened because God knew I that would get through it and fight harder than I ever did in my life...and that this fight would be worth sharing with people who need to hear it...that my story could inspire other people to fight too." He waited to see what she would say, afraid his thinking was flawed in some way, that he hadn't found his purpose yet. He needed her feedback before he could believe in it because she had seen so clearly through to his soul so many times.

"I love that so much," she said, and Ben felt his anxiety melt away. "I know your fight will help so many people."

"Thank you. That means so much to me."

"You're welcome." She reached behind her where she had hidden the item from her hand. "I got you something that I thought you'd like. My mother and I go to the gift shop once in a while to see if there is anything new. It's not much, but I thought about you when I saw it." Finally, she extended her arm and opened her hand to him, revealing a small wooden cross carved in an odd form. It wasn't a traditional straight up-and-down cross but instead curved and bent. It was formed perfectly for his paralyzed hands.

He took it gently and turned it over, examining the odd shape.

She explained, "It's a clinging cross! It's supposed to be helpful for people who struggle with using their hands. If you practice holding it, it'll improve your grip."

"Thank you so much!" he exclaimed.

She gently took his hand in hers and guided his fingers to close around the cross. When his hand twitched and the cross fell to the floor, she patiently picked it up and started again.

A few minutes later, there was a knock at the door, and a voice called, "Mr. Norwood, I have your lunch for today. Can I come in?"

"Absolutely!" Ben called back, laying aside the cross.

An older lady, whom Ben had not seen before, came in and set a tray down on the bedside table and turned it so that it lay over his lap. "There you go," she said in a grandmotherly way before leaving. Ben normally received feeding services, but it seemed she didn't know, and Ben was too embarrassed to call her back.

Ben uncovered the plate to find chopped steak in brown gravy, mashed potatoes, and green beans. His stomach rumbled. "Have you eaten yet?" He asked Penny.

"I can't eat until dinner. They're doing a blood test later today. I'm not hungry anyway. You go ahead!"

Ben slowly reached for his fork, and as his fingers closed around it, his hand twitched into the side of the tray and knocked over a little carton of butter. He scooped up some mash potatoes, but on the way to his mouth, his arm flailed and sent the potatoes past his ear. He sighed.

"Can I help?" Penny asked hesitantly, remembering his embarrassment the last time.

Ben swallowed his pride once again and nodded.

She lowered his bed to make it easier to reach him. They sat there for a while as she slowly guided his hand with each bite to his mouth and talked. Duke occasionally got up from his nap to check on his lovebirds and then laid his head back down.

"You're like a guardian angel," Ben said to her when they were nearly done. "I'm so grateful to have you in my life. You keep showing me what I can accomplish with strength, faith, and a positive mindset. Even here, you're helping me eat, but I noticed you're not taking over the movement completely.

You're letting my muscles relearn how to eat. I want to tell you how much you mean to me. You'll always have a special place in my heart."

"And you'll always live in mine, Ben," Penelope whispered, tears in her eyes. "But I haven't been doing anything special. Mostly just hanging out with you."

Ben proceeded to tell her about how his childhood friend Brandon had relieved his depression by "just hanging out with him." He smiled and took another bite. "I think just being there unconditionally for someone in a troubling time is the most powerful tool against anger, depression, and loneliness. I want to be there for *you* in that way too."

That night, Ben lay in bed and thought of his life once again. Everything seemed to be falling back into place...a new place, yes, but perhaps a better place. So many good things were happening: all of the gains he had been making, his general attitude and mental health, the new foundation of faith he was establishing, and the relationship that he was building with Penelope. He was beginning to see the purpose behind everything and building up confidence and trust in God's plan. Every moment he spent with Penny drew them closer to each other. He spent some time in an elaborate daydream of himself proposing to her even though they had known each other for only a month. He felt at peace.

CHAPTER 17

G od is not punishing those who live with chronic illness. He is creating warriors who learn through the storms and in turn come to a way of helping others. A warrior of God will face fear but learn to have the courage to turn that fear into faith. For Ben, there were days when the fear made him think it would be best to stay in bed. But that was not God's plan for Ben's life.

A few days had passed since Penny's last visit, and Ben began to worry. He had stopped at her door several times, but she hadn't been in. He played out all the scenarios in his head of where she was, thinking surely someone would have told him if something bad had happened to her. He would have heard alarms and rushing nurses from the hallway if she had coded, the term Ben had learned meant needing immediate life-saving medical attention.

He looked over to one of the verses she had put on his wall. "*Philippians 4:6–7 Do not be anxious about anything, but in everything by prayer and supplication with thanksgiving, let your requests be made known to God. And the peace of God, which surpasses all understanding, will guard your hearts and your minds in Christ Jesus.*" He took a deep breath and felt that peace fill him. He then felt an urge to visit her room. "God's timing," he told himself.

He pushed the button to call for help getting into his chair, which turned out to be his easiest transfer yet. Ben was getting much stronger, able to support more and more of his weight. However, he had been instructed to still use his wheelchair to be safe. Once he was situated in his chair, he shuffled out into the hallway. He felt at peace looking at her door, but he said a silent prayer, asking for the courage to face what he was about to find in her room. He knocked but did not hear anything. Gently, he cracked the door open. "Hello?" he called softly. "Is it okay to come in?"

A very weak voice came from inside. "Yes, Benny."

He opened the door wider and entered. His heart began to race at seeing her. She had a slight bluish tint to her skin, and she looked barely conscious as she lay in bed looking at him. Duke had crawled into bed next to her. As soon as he approached her bed, he heard footsteps come in behind him and turned to find Penny's mother.

She explained to Ben that the doctors had been searching far and wide for donor lungs to perform the transplant, but they were losing hope as Penny was losing time. They looked over to Penny, who had closed her eyes. Her mother whispered, "No one can tell me how much longer she'll live without a transplant, but…" She trailed off, eyes glued to the face of her daughter.

Ben was filled with so many different emotions that he didn't know what to do. He grabbed her hands and found them very cold.

She opened her eyes again, looked into Ben's, and smiled reassuringly. Ben had to lean in to hear her faint voice as she said, "It's going to be okay, my sweet Benny. I am in pain and very tired, but I am about to go to a place of no pain very soon…a place filled with love, peace, and happiness. My body is tired, and I am ready to go home to see the wonderful Heaven."

Ben opted out of all his therapy that day to stay with her. Her mom eventually had to go home to take care of a few things and said she would be back later to stay the night. Ben watched a romantic comedy movie, while Penny went in and out of sleep. Every once in a while, he would find Penny awake long enough to watch a full scene, and occasionally, her lips curved into a small smile. Twice, she even laughed. She sniffled and wiped her eyes at a sad part. Apparently, she liked movies like this. There was still so much he didn't know about her.

That evening would forever be engraved in his heart and memory: her smiles, tears, and laughter. When the movie was over, Ben began speaking to her. He shared more of his passions, dreams, and past events in his life. After a while, she closed her eyes again, but he kept talking. "I always had a particular dream of what I wanted: Living in a little home because I never felt like I needed a mansion. Married to the love of my life. Having two kids, one boy and one girl. They could be my blood or adopted, it didn't matter. I just wanted to be a better father than my father was. Making enough money to comfortably pay the bills. Putting away a little for the kids' college funds and spoiling my wife every once in a while. Yeah. I know it wouldn't always be rainbows and happy times, but I still want that."

As he was imagining this old dream, the blank wife figure that had been a placeholder for so long was now replaced with Penny. He would buy her romantic comedy books and movies. They would build a garden together. They would take their children to the beach and ride a train across the countryside. It was the most beautiful dream he had ever had, and he knew it was impossible.

Later that evening, Ben had lapsed into brooding silence when Penny's mom returned. He said goodbye to Penelope, who awoke with another small smile. He held tightly to her hand, trying to hold back the tears that were forcing their way from his eyes. "I'll see you soon, Penny," he said. "We still need to go see the prayer garden."

She nodded, then fell back asleep.

Ben lay in his bed that night, staring at the ceiling in a state of helplessness and grief. He couldn't stop the tears or the dark thoughts. When his whole body began shaking, he sat up in a panic, looking wildly around the room for something to ground him. He found the verses Penny had put on his walls, and one in particular caught his attention: *John 3:16 "For God so loved the world that he gave his one and only Son, that whoever believes in him shall not perish but have eternal life."* He prayed until he fell asleep, hours later.

CHAPTER 18

I t was two in the morning when it happened. Ben was awoken by a dog barking, followed quickly by a loud machine shrilling and doctors and nurses running past his room.

A moment later, he heard commands being shouted and statuses being called out. Penelope was flat-lining. Ben gathered they were giving her injections and hooking her up to machines.

They tried. For over an hour, they tried. When everything went quiet, Ben knew it was done.

A nurse looked into his room a few minutes later and noticed he was awake and crying. She came in and said, "I'm sorry. We couldn't get her heart to restart. She was just ready to go on."

He lay in a daze the rest of the day. He seemed to have run out of tears. When breakfast and lunch arrived, he couldn't eat. His stomach felt tight and sore. He didn't talk much to anyone. Jules came by at dinner to comfort him and coax him into eating a few bites. He drifted off into a floaty, dreamless sleep that night.

When Jules came back the following morning, she asked him whether he was up for therapy. He just shrugged his shoulders. She took that for agreement and helped move him to his chair. She took him down to the gym and talked about how staying in bed would not help him, how a day spent lying down cost five days of hard exercise to keep up with progress., and how getting up and moving would help him recover from his friend's death. They went through simple review activities. Ben did them all successfully but spoke as little as possible.

The next three days passed in a blur, where each day seemed to repeat the last. It seemed it would go on forever this way, but on the fourth day, he was informed that his insurance was ready to discharge him from the hospital. Jules came to see him off.

"I'm so proud of you, Ben," she said as she hugged him goodbye. "You've come such a long way."

"Your support has meant so much to me. And I'm sure your secret nighttime prayers helped too," Ben grinned.

"Oh! You know about that? I hope that's okay. I often do that for patients who are struggling."

"It was a comfort knowing you believed in me even when I didn't."

He would still need a wheelchair for long excursions, but he was able to move around for the most part without it. The day after he had arrived home, he got a phone call from Penelope's mom, letting him know about the funeral and requesting Ben to say a eulogy.

He stayed up that whole night, stewing in so many emotions and trying to organize his thoughts. By this time, he could very slowly type on his computer, something he had not done in so long. Now he used his re-learned skills to compose what he hoped was a most beautiful eulogy. After he finished it, he realized what he was doing felt right. Not just expressing his feelings for Penny but the *writing*. He opened a new document and began telling the story of his life and how he had met Penelope.

And as he wrote, Ben began to explore the purpose of it all. He could see a thousand pieces of his shattered heart all over the place, but he thought he could also see God picking them up, one by one, and putting them back together. He knew that it would take time, but that one day, he would be able to move on, carrying her in his heart forever, just as he had promised her. He would have to learn to love again, just as he had to relearn how to do everything else from walking to eating and tying his shoes. This was the building of a warrior, Ben thought: a warrior who would be strong enough to lead others to believe in God and look to him more.

The following Saturday, Ben and his mother drove back to San Antonio for a celebration of Penny's life. The church was large and covered in beautiful stained-glass windows. One of them resembled the one in the hospital chapel that he and Penny had looked at together. When he saw this, he felt like God was winking at him to let him know that it was going to be okay. The place was filled with people, those who knew Penny but whom Ben had never got to meet. Ben and his mother sat near the back where there was an open spot for wheelchairs.

The service was beautiful. There were amazing pieces of music and wonderful readings of the word of God. The service was a true celebration of life. When the pastor at the podium said, "Now we will have Benjamin Norwood share some words about Penelope," Ben began rolling up the aisle in his wheelchair. On the way, people peered back to look at him. Among the faces, Ben saw Duane. He had a sad little smile on his face that clearly said his heart was breaking for Ben.

At the front, Ben spotted Jules and Penny's family. Duke was with them, looking a little lost. Avee and Haleigh and their mother were there too. The girls were still wearing their glittery neck braces. Avee had one arm draped over Duke's shoulders.

There was no ramp up to the podium, so Ben set the breaks on his wheels and pushed himself up, his speech in one hand. Jules popped up next to him, hovering to make sure he didn't fall. He swayed on the first step but caught himself and managed to keep his balance up the next two steps. Jules followed him up and stayed next to him like a protective mother of a toddler learning to walk. Ben supposed it wasn't so dissimilar.

He stood there for a few moments, just staring at the crowd and gathering up all his emotions. He felt he had reached a peaceful place, but this would be the first time he would talk about her since her death. And he was going to be doing it in front of so many people, most of whom had known her longer than he had. He began speaking.

"Hello, everyone. My name is Benjamin Norwood, and I met Penny at the hospital. I had major brain surgery, which unexpectedly left me a quadriplegic. I was told that I would have to relearn everything from the neck down, and I was in a very dark place mentally. I was ready to give up on myself and God.

"Then I met Penny. She helped me discover the purpose of my life. She became the source of my determination to keep trying. I may have hit rock bottom, but Penny showed me that I had found the foundation on which to build my faith stronger than ever! When I was wallowing in self-pity, wondering, 'Why me?' Penny taught me that there was purpose in everything that had happened to me. When I could not feed myself or walk, she gave me the strength to stand up and try. When I felt alone and tired and in pain, she said that God is with us every moment, rooting us on as we struggle. I learned from her that we must continue to fight, no matter what, and that God has a plan for us. Meeting Penny was in God's plan for me, just as I know she was in all of your lives for a purpose as well.

"She was a warrior who fought hard for life and for her loved ones, but now she is where there is no war. Now she can live in a place without pain and suffering. She's left us now physically, but we will forever carry the strength she gave us. And one day, we will be with her again in Heaven. Let us always remember the great impact she had on all our lives. Thank you."

Many people were crying and dabbing their eyes as Ben stepped carefully down the steps and returned to his chair. He rolled back down the aisle to watch the rest of the service and then traveled by car with the rest to the burial.

After everything was complete, he asked his mother, "Can we please go visit the hospital?" Once they arrived, his mother got the wheelchair out, and Ben got on.

She pushed him through the front doors and then asked, "Where to?"

"You'll see. Just follow me," Ben smiled. He began shuffling along down the hallway and looking at the directional signs. He turned a corner too quickly and almost ran over a stalky Hispanic man. It was Mario.

"Woah there, turbo!" Mario said as he leaped out of the way "I see you're getting around pretty well now. How have you been?"

So, Ben filled him in about his life-changing miracle of walking again ("I only use the wheelchair for long trips") but could not summon the strength to talk about Penny. He wanted to match the upbeat personality that Mario had.

Ben's mother jokingly told Mario, "I know you see many patients, so I don't know if you remember, but you once told my son you were going to salsa with him!"

Mario's eyes lit up, and he said, "You are right!" And with a show of his strength as a strong and talented physical therapist, he scooped Ben right out of his chair. He gently positioned Ben's feet on top of his own, and they danced the salsa together in that little hallway. Everyone was laughing and filled with joy. His mom even shed a little tear.

"Okay, my friends," Mario said after a few minutes of this. "I am running a little late to see a patient. I need to go! It was so great seeing you both." He helped Ben back into his chair and walked off briskly.

"Aren't you going to tell me where we're going?" his mother asked after another few minutes of navigating the maze of the hospital.

"It's a place I need to see," Ben responded. "Penny said she would take me there, but..." He trailed off into silence for a moment. "Almost there." He found the door he was looking for and stood up to push it open. He held the door open for his mother and followed her in.

It was the prayer garden. It was just as beautiful as he remembered from the windows. There were bright flowers and green leaves, warm sunlight in the open areas, and cool shadows under the trees. There was a young lady sitting on one of the benches under the tree. She was blond, wore glasses, and appeared to be praying and meditating.

"It's so beautiful!" his mom exclaimed." She leaned in to smell the closest flowers as Ben moved past her. She must have understood that he needed to walk alone here as she didn't follow him.

After struggling to safely find his balance on the slightly uneven terrain, he made his way to another cement bench. As his gaze slowly roamed over the garden, he felt the great sadness of missing Penny well up again. Tears once again coursed their way down his cheeks, but he just let them come this time instead of trying to fight them. After a while, the flood slowed to a trickle, and he began to sniffle and look for tissue in his pockets.

His hands ran into something hard and smooth. He pulled out the clinging cross that Penny had gifted him. Seeing this sent him into an even deeper reflection of what has happened and what was to happen. Living a life without her would be difficult, he knew, but there would always be reminders, things keeping her alive with him, such as this cross. God provides opportunities at every moment in life, and Ben would seek out all the joys of life in as many different ways as possible. All the emotions finally collapsed into a fathomless well of sadness, loss, a little bit of hope, and some confusion, sending yet more tears down his face.

He heard the sound of crunching leaves and looked up. The woman who had been sharing the garden with him was approaching hesitantly. He gave her a slight smile and wiped his face on his sleeves, which she seemed to take for an invitation, for she sat next to him before handing him a packet of tissues.

"Hi. My name is Sarah. I'm one of the chaplains for the hospital."

"Thanks, I'm Benny," he said, taking the tissues gratefully.

"Are you a patient here?" she asked.

"I was until recently. I had to come back here to...well, it's a long story."

"Oh! Do you feel comfortable sharing your story with me?" Before he could answer, she looked down at his other hand and spotted the clinging cross. She gestured toward it and said, "Also, I love your clinging cross!"

Ben was the type of person who was comfortable talking to anyone, so he told her the craziest story of his life, starting with the pain he had felt and ignored from childhood and leading all the way up to this very moment and the reason why he was crying in this prayer garden. He felt a weight lift after talking about it. He thought the well of overwhelming emotion wasn't quite as endless.

Sarah's eyes had teared up, and she said, "Your friend...Penelope...she sounds like an amazing woman. I would love to have met her. Do you know if she was saved?" He looked at her in confusion.

She then explained, "To be saved means that you invite Jesus Christ into your heart and have a personal relationship with God."

Ben replied, "Well, I never asked her, but I'm pretty sure she was!"

She then said something that resonated well with Ben. "You see, everything on this earth is temporary—your body and all the things that come in your life. God never promised there would be no pain or sadness while we are here. He does, however, say to look to him and trust him in those times. God is with us in the fire, and all we have to do is have faith and stand in his love. I believe that Penelope is in Heaven in her eternal body, living in a place of no pain and free of cystic fibrosis."

Although Ben had been a Christian his whole life, he felt he had been experiencing everything lately in a new way—in his new faith. He had been learning a new kind of relationship with God. "I want to be saved too," Ben told Sarah. "I've never been ready before, but now...I understand."

"That's wonderful!" Sarah exclaimed. "You can do that right here, right now! All you have to do is say it. Repeat after me if you're ready."

Ben nodded. "I invite Jesus Christ into my heart to guide me as my Lord and Savior."

Ben repeated the words, feeling his heart opening and expanding and being filled with holy light. The garden took on an even brighter and more beautiful glow. He felt light and unburdened. He smiled at Sarah.

"Now, just because you are saved doesn't mean no bad things will come your way. In fact, the devil will come around more now that you're escaping him, and he'll hit you from all directions, trying to distract you from the works God has for you. However, you must never forget to chase after God's heart in every situation. People will fail you, but God will never fail you." She looked at her watch and jumped up. "I've lost track of the time. It was lovely to meet you, Ben. You can stay as long as you want and let it all sink in."

Ben watched her go. He remained on the bench for nearly an hour, reflecting on his journey and, finally, considering the future. His path forward seemed clearer than ever. Benjamin Norwood was going to use his story to show the world the love and power of God and the importance of never giving up. He began crying again, but this time, they were tears of happiness. He knew that no matter what came his way, from now on, God would be there with him. He glanced up to the windows from which he and Penelope had looked down on this garden together. He could see Penelope smiling down on him, and he smiled back through the tears.

AFTERWORD

I felt like I needed to explain a few things since this book is based on my life. There are situations in this book that will make you wonder how in the world I came up with them. Nearly everything in this book is either exactly as it happened to me or is inspired by something in my life.

First, I chose the name Benjamin in honor of my cousin, who has autism. The name can be shortened just like my own name (Matthew to Matt). The last name Norwood belongs to my mother's family.

The bullying Ben went through early in life is from a part of my life that I don't speak about much maybe because I reacted differently from some people. I really tried to suffer in silence and not show people that I was hurting. I did have plenty of episodes of extreme depression, but very few people knew about it. I was always teased about the size of my head and told that the level of niceness I showed was "creepy." I could just throw the excuse out that "kids are mean," and, I mean they are, but throwing this excuse down is like slapping a Band-Aid on a serious issue. I included these scenes to raise awareness of the effects bullying have on the mental health of victims.

For men specifically, I want to make mental illness just as important as physical illness because in our society, we as men live by this unspoken rule that we are not allowed to speak up. Society may tell you it is not manly to say you are hurting emotionally, but I believe this is a lie that needs to fade away.

Ben lands a huge movie role, which is something I almost did...I won't say which Disney movie, but I auditioned for a casting director with whom I became great friends. She most likely won't remember who I am now. Anyway, I auditioned for the lead role's onscreen boyfriend. I found out through this friend that it was down to me and another boy in Washington state. He got the role.

Ben going into the military is another thing that *almost* happened to me. I was talking to a marine recruiter, and I was so close to "signing the dotted line" when, at the last minute, I changed my mind. I wanted to add this part as a "what if" moment because I wanted to explore what might have happened if I had actually joined the Marines. I think I most likely would have been diagnosed while attending boot camp, and I also thought it would be an interesting way for Ben to receive his diagnosis.

The way Ben gets injured at boot camp was inspired by a brawl I had with a friend. Duane is portraying a friend of mine, Sage. He and I got into a fist fight one time, and he hit me in the back of the head. It was way before my diagnosis. He absolutely wouldn't have done that knowing what I had going on. I have since forgiven him.

I am big on practicing what you preach, and I preach forgiveness in a big way. For some reason, I was blessed with an extreme amount of forgiveness and patience. I love my fellow humans. What kind of man would I be if I didn't forgive someone? Forgiving is probably one of the strongest weapons you have against the devil. You have that power inside you!

Ben went to San Antonio and met his doctor in just about the way I did, and the doctor also closely portrays my previous doctor.

When I bring up Ehlers-Danlos Syndrome, it is because I want to spread awareness about it and because I believe I have this co-condition even though I haven't been diagnosed with it.

The therapists that Ben deals with all portray real therapists that I have met through my journey. For example, I actually was told by a therapist that we were going to learn how to salsa dance, but I was released from the hospital the day after he said this. I later re-visited the hospital and found him again. At first, he didn't recognize me. I had already gained so much weight since he last saw me and was wearing street clothes instead of a hospital gown.

After talking to him for a few minutes to refresh his memory, I brought up what he had said about the salsa dancing. Without a moment of hesitation, he grabbed my hands, propped my feet on his feet, and danced with me in that hallway. I will never forget this moment. It still gives me goosebumps and inspiration. It probably didn't mean that much to him, but I am literally getting teary eyed just retelling this story.

Whenever I dove into a deeper telling of my story through Benjamin, I tried to get even more raw and real with you than I had with my memoir. I tried to really show the deep struggle I had with good and evil as I fought to get my life back. I am a very positive-minded man and will most likely be that way to my grave. In *Faith Over Fear*, I chose to really focus on my lighthearted side of things. However, I guess through fiction, I wanted to show you the darker emotions I went through.

The character Penelope is a fictional character in many ways, but some parts of her portray a woman I was with during my surgery and early recovery. We have parted ways, and that was why I had Penelope die in the end. It was in a very strange way a last emotional letting go of her. When

Penelope died, it was the feeling I had when my previous relationship had ended.

Some of the things Penelope did and the way she was such an encouragement to Ben are exactly how I felt in the relationship I had. For example, she and my mother put scripture around my room, which truly helped me. I am now a happily married man to a beautiful woman named Hannah. She blesses me every day, and I am even working on a book a lot like this on how we met.

A little spoiler alert: I am working on a book that continues the story of one of the side characters that are in this book, but I don't want to say who.

Please read all the testimonials after this and see other people who are fighting the good fight. Be reminded to not take things for granted and to enjoy even the smallest of things in life. You are an incredible and strong human being with extraordinary skills. Don't ever think that you don't matter, and most importantly...You are enough! So, don't stop fighting.

Lara Bloom: President & CEO of The EDS society

My name is Lara Bloom, and I'm the President & CEO of The Ehlers-Danlos Society, responsible for globally raising awareness of rare, chronic and invisible diseases, specializing in the Ehlers-Danlos syndromes, hypermobility spectrum disorders (HSD) and associated symptoms and conditions.

My journey with EDS began at the age of 11 when I began showing symptoms such as chronic pain and fatigue, recurrent pneumonias and chest infections, endometriosis, polycystic ovaries, as well as breathing issues due to a pectus excavatum. There was a long 12-year odyssey of misdiagnosis, people not believing me, being called a hypochondriac and being bounced from doctor to doctor before I was diagnosed with EDS at the age of 24. I have most of the multi-systemic features, including some other rarer ones that aren't always typical with hEDS, as well as quite a few marfanoid habitus physical attributes.

The biggest thing that affects me are my autonomic issues, although they are well managed now with medication, regular exercise and a good diet. I still suffer with the issues that come with EDS every day; I currently have a big tear in my right glute, a labral tear in my right hip, a meniscus tear in my left knee as well as a tendon tear in my right ankle. The thing that has made the biggest impact in my quality of life is that I now take a very high dose of vitamins, exercise on average of four times a week, as when the muscle strength increases with EDS, it can really help. However, it is vital to respect the condition. I make sure not to push myself too hard in terms of stamina; I keep cardio limited, concentrating on strength building doing closed chain exercises. Also, thinking about tips and tricks that help with traveling, I always go with an iPad instead of a laptop, and I check-in a bag instead of carrying one so I don't have to lift anything heavy upwards, as well as keeping well hydrated and taking extra electrolytes.

I think it's hard to have a condition that's invisible; people don't always see the pain you're going through, but sometimes it is also nice to have the ability to walk around without any visible signs of that pain. My hope is that everyone out there with these kinds of conditions allows themselves to have their bad days but almost more importantly, to thrive in their good days. I'm lucky to be blessed with a wonderful family, great friends, a fluffy white dog and being able to see the world while working with some incredible colleagues. I think life is a gift we should appreciate and enjoy every day, even when some of those days can be incredibly hard and frustrating. I am very fortunate to be doing something so fulfilling. Making a difference is incredibly rewarding, and I feel very privileged and grateful to be doing this work.

For those of you with EDS and HSD, I'd like to say the road ahead is brightly paved with optimism and positivity. This condition has historically been neglected in terms of funding, research and collaboration. With the launch of The Ehlers-Danlos Society, there is now a global organisation that's there and dedicated to finding the funds needed for research to facilitate the continuing global collaboration needed to keep driving this progression. We won't stop until wealth or geography no longer dictates your quality life living with EDS and HSD.

Ashley Wilson: 21/Cystic Fibrosis

Hi! My name is Ashley Wilson. I am a curious 21-year-old who enjoys hiking, surfing, traveling, and always wanting to try something new. I am currently in college studying film production to work in the film industry. My dream is to make documentaries. My love of creating videos began when I started my YouTube channel, "Ashley's Roses," in 2016. I wanted to share my perspective on living with cystic fibrosis and make a positive impact on those who watch my videos.

There are many things that make up one person. Whether that is playing a sport, where you were raised, or different experiences you have had. Cystic fibrosis is only a portion of me; it does not define me, but it has shaped me to be the person I am today.

I was born in Denver, Colorado and diagnosed with cystic fibrosis at birth. Colorado was the first state in the nation to include cystic fibrosis in newborn screening. From a young age, cystic fibrosis affected my digestive system and my lungs; however, as I became older, CF began to affect me in other areas. I later moved to California in 2006 and noticed how well my lungs adjusted to living near the salty air of the ocean.In 2011, I was diagnoses with Cystic Fibrosis Related Diabetes. This was a shock for me at first because I never thought I would have to experience taking insulin. Overtime, I began to get used to my new routine with taking insulin. In 2015, I was diagnosed with Cystic Fibrosis Liver Disease. I never saw this coming. At this time of the year, I was the healthiest I had ever been and before I knew it, I was being rushed to the hospital. They discovered I had CF Liver Disease because I was bleeding internally in my esophagus. The blood could not flow through my liver and backed up to my esophagus. They had to perform a TIPS Procedure, seal up the bleeding vessels, and put me on the liver transplant list. A TIPS Procedure is when they put a shunt, which is a tiny tube, in the artery to help with the blood flow. I was in the hospital for a month with a long and slow recovery. I have learned from CF that things can be thrown your way and that sometimes there is no way to be prepared. Since then, I have been taken off the transplant list, and my liver been stable since that time.

That is only a small glance of what I have experienced from living with cystic fibrosis. I am only 21 years old, yet I have experienced more than the average person. There are moments of joy, sadness, and fear when living with CF. It is easy to wonder what will come next when battling this illness, but I have learned over the years that in doing that, you are letting the what-ifs stop you from truly living your life. Learn to treasure each day and take risks.—risks of living your life to the fullest because you are never guaranteed tomorrow. Each day you have and each breath that you take is a blessing.

Julie Jandeska: 22/Arnold Chiari Malformation

My name is Julie Jandeska, and I am a 22-year-old from Illinois. I was diagnosed with Chiari Malformation when I was 20. Prior to that, I was diagnosed with scoliosis, which is associated with Chiari Malformation. Around when I was in 6th grade, I was always sick, and no one could explain why. I finally was taken to a doctor who cared, and I was told that my spine was curved in an "s" shape which was pushing my internal organs into each other. I finally had an answer as to why I was always sick, but what were the treatment options? My options were to go the traditional route and get a rod put in my spine to correct the curve, or I would work on building up my core muscles which would then straighten my spine. I chose to build my core muscles by starting horseback riding in 7th grade, and I have been riding ever since. I have been riding for almost 10 years now, and it has changed my life for the better. My spine is as straight as it will ever be, but I was still having issues. I was not feeling as sick anymore, but I was still having plenty of other issues.

Some of these issues included having a shooting and stabbing pain going through my right hip, balance problems, not being able to feel the right half of my torso, having issues regulating my body's temperature, and even more symptoms. I went to a hip doctor, and they told me that I had a torn labrum. I was in my sophomore year in college when I got the hip surgery right before Christmas. After I healed from that surgery, the pain in my hip never stopped, and no one could explain it. I put off going back to any doctors for a year, but I was finally convinced to go back to a doctor when I had come back from a run and the right half of my body was freezing cold while the left half of my body was hot and sweaty just as it should be after a run. I was then referred to a neurologist and then made an appointment.

After the first appointment, I was referred to get MRIs of my spine and my brain with and without contrast. The results showed that I had Chiari Malformation and Syringomyelia. This was not something that I took well, and I really did not believe the doctor. I went on to get a second opinion, which ended up with the same diagnosis. Shortly after that, I was sched-uled for decompression surgery July 31st, 2017. I was so sick of being in constant pain, and I just wanted it to be over. The constant headaches, the numbness of the right half of my body, the shooting pains—everything; I was tired of everything. I scheduled surgery for the day after I got back from a trip to Colorado, and I was ready for the pain to be over.

I had the decompression surgery the summer before my junior year in college. I remember going into the hospital and being terrified to have the surgery but also excited to not be in constant pain anymore. I woke up from surgery and remember being in a tremendous amount of pain. They wanted to do an MRI post operation to see how it looked, and I could not move my head because I was in so much pain. I remember thinking, "Oh boy, another MRI," because I had had over 20 MRIs done on me the past year. They moved my head for me to get the MRI, and then I went to the intensive care floor for the night. I was in the hospital for 2 days, and then I went home to start the recovery process. It took roughly 6 months to fully heal from the surgery, but the surgery did not really do much. I still have the numbness, the headaches, the balance issues, chronic pain, etc., and I am still searching for answers. Chiari effects people in different ways, and I feel as if I am still in an uphill battle with all of my symptoms. But the only thing I can do is try to get through each day with a smile on my face. I still have a ton of unanswered questions, but I will continue to conquer Chiari and not let it conquer me.

Rachel: 22/Chiari and EDS

Hi! Before I tell you my story, let me introduce myself. My name is Rachel. I'm twenty-two years old, a CrossFitter, fitness enthusiast, musician, and born with Chiari Malformation and Ehlers Danlos Syndrome. From the time I was two and a half years old, I suffered from daily headaches. It was a life I had grown to be used to. I went through most of my childhood without ever knowing why I experienced headaches and why I always seemed to be different from my siblings and friends. When I was ten years old, I started to have some trouble with my eyes, which led to a brain MRI and discovering my

Chiari Malformation. At the time, I was told it was just a coincidental finding, there was nothing to do or worry about, and I just had migraines. Over the next nine years, I dealt with a variety of symptoms and conditions, which all tied back to Chiari and EDS and ultimately led to the decision being made to go through with decompression surgery. It was during this process that we discovered I also had Ehlers Danlos Syndrome. Getting this diagnosis felt like the missing piece to a lifelong puzzle. This journey has not been an easy one, but I have learned that even when I can't see it, there is a greater plan in place for me. The initial years of my diagnoses and recovery after surgery were tough. I struggled a lot with understanding why I was chosen to go along this path and why I was bearing this burden and not someone else.

Along my journey, I found CrossFit and weightlifting, and it became a great passion of mine. When I was diagnosed with Chiari, I was never told that I shouldn't lift heavy weights or ride rollercoasters. When my symptoms began to worsen in my late teen years, I was told that I would have to stop the thing I loved most. This was a moment when I really questioned my faith—I wondered why I couldn't just be like everyone else. I was frustrated and angry with the plan for me. I didn't want that for my life. But as I have grown, both in age and in my faith, I have discovered that there is a greater plan for me than I can even know. While there are days when these conditions feel like too heavy a burden to keep going on, I'm reminded that there is a purpose to my journey. Today, that purpose is getting to share a little bit of my story. To whomever is reading this, let this be a reminder: You are never alone.

Heidi Taylor: Arnold Chiari Malformation

On November 1, 2017, I woke up at 3 a.m. to drink the second half of the liquid needed for my colonoscopy scheduled for later that day. When I woke up, I had a headache across the top of my eyes that brought me to the floor in so much pain. Later, I was told that was my first migraine. It eventually subsided after about an hour. I had my scheduled colonoscopy later that day and began to have this headache that was very dull all the time.

In December, I asked my primary care doctor to do something about my headaches. She ordered a CT scan. She said that it came back normal and that I was just under stress. I continued working as a preschool teacher, but after the holidays, I was having a constant headache that was starting to affect my daily life. I asked my primary care doctor for a referral to a neurologist.

At the end of January, I saw a neurologist, and she ordered an MRI. When the results came in, she called me in to see her. She told me three words I had never heard of before. Chiari 1 malformation. She ordered another contrast/non-contrast MRI and an MRA. She also ordered a spinal scan. I went back to see the neurologist after all the tests were back in: 7 mm measurement of a malformation. The malformation was not seen on the CT scan by my regular doctor, but the neurologist saw it. My headaches were constant at this point and brought dizziness and forgetfulness. I continued working and was told that decompression surgery would help. I was scheduled to see a neurosurgeon. I had no idea what was happening in my brain. Why would I have this? What would it mean? How would my life change? Brain surgery? Would I ever be normal again?

Fast forward to the meeting of a neurosurgeon in March 2018. My husband went with me, and the doctor explained what he would be doing and that I had a 70% chance that it would help relieve my symptoms. He also told me that I would be in a world of pain when I woke up from surgery. He was surprised that I was still working. Only by God's strength. April 10th would be my surgery date. I have never had any major surgeries in my life. I was 43 years old at the time. The surgery date fast approached, and the pressure headaches were getting more and more severe. They kept me from sleeping, and they kept me from functioning anything near my previous normal. I had asked for prayer from my church, family, and anyone who would be willing to pray for me.

The surgery date came. Doctor said surgery was successful. I woke up from surgery in ICU feeling like someone had hit me across the back of my neck with a baseball bat. I remained in ICU overnight and then was moved to a room. I stayed three days in the hospital, mainly in shock, but the headache pressure was not there. I had 20 staples in the back of my head. I left the hospital and remained off work for 2 months. I kept asking the doctors what normal recovery would look like and how I could help heal faster and be able to live my old life faster. There were never any answers, there was no research, and the doctors didn't know. The frustration of having Chiari 1 and a chronic illness set in.

It has been almost a year since surgery. I have noticed that my vision, which used to be good, is starting to get worse—blurry when I am trying to read. I also have accepted the fact that I need to write things down as my once good memory is not that good anymore. My short-term memory has been affected. My stamina is also slower now. I have days that I feel good, but they are very few. There is also some type of soreness in my neck always. I start my day with a heat pack on my neck, ice in the afternoon, and ice at night. But the pressure headaches were gone. Grateful.

This past February, I was in a car accident; my husband ran into the back of the car in front of us. This triggered something as I am having the burning headaches again. The pressure headache has returned but not as severe. The doctors want me to try the medicines that didn't work pre-surgery last year. I truly believe at this point that the accident triggered me to have symptoms again. I am not willing to live on pain medicine the rest of my life. I have a life to live. Chiari won't win.

Matthew Lemke was diagnosed with an incurable brain disorder called
Arnold Chiari malformation, and he also had a rare spinal cyst called
syringomyelia.
After facing an incredible obstacle after his surgery, he decided to put his
faith in God and defeat his fear. Today, Matthew is married to his beautiful
wife, and they have a handsome son.
He is an author, photographer, and motivational speaker sharing with
others what Jesus has done in his life so far. Matthew is also a seminary
student while working a full-time job. His hope is to show people that God
is still in the miracle business and that we should never give up under any
circumstance.